PIANO LESSONS
CAN BE MURDER

PIANO LESSONS
CAN BE MURDER

R.L. STINE

SCHOLASTIC INC.
New York Toronto London Auckland Sydney
Mexico City New Delhi Hong Kong Buenos Aires

1

I thought I was going to hate moving into a new house. But actually, I had fun.

I played a pretty mean joke on Mom and Dad.

While they were busy in the front room showing the moving men where to put stuff, I went exploring. I found a really neat room to the side of the dining room.

It had big windows on two sides looking out onto the back yard. Sunlight poured in, making the room brighter and a lot more cheery than the rest of the old house.

The room was going to be our new family room. You know, with a TV and CD player, and maybe a Ping-Pong table and stuff. But right now it was completely empty.

Except for two gray balls of dust in one corner, which gave me an idea.

Chuckling to myself, I bent down and shaped the two dust balls with my hands. Then I began shouting in a real panicky voice: "Mice! Mice! Help! *Mice!*"

Mom and Dad came bursting into the room at the same time. Their mouths nearly dropped to the floor when they saw the two gray dust mice.

I kept screaming, "Mice! Mice!" Pretending I was scared of them. Trying hard to keep a straight face.

Mom just stood in the doorway, her mouth hanging open. I really thought she was going to drop her teeth!

Dad always panics more than Mom. He picked up a broom that was leaning against the wall, ran across the room, and began pounding the poor, defenseless dust mice with it.

By that time, I was laughing my head off.

Dad stared down at the glob of dust stuck to the end of the broom, and he finally caught on it was a joke. His face got real red, and I thought his eyes were going to pop out from behind his glasses.

"Very funny, Jerome," Mom said calmly, rolling her eyes. Everyone calls me Jerry, but she calls me Jerome when she's upset with me. "Your father and I sure appreciate your scaring us to death when we're both very nervous and overworked and trying to get moved into this house."

Mom is always real sarcastic like that. I think

2

I probably get my sense of humor from her.

Dad just scratched the bald spot on the back of his head. "They really looked like mice," he muttered. He wasn't angry. He's used to my jokes. They both are.

"Why can't you act your age?" Mom asked, shaking her head.

"I am!" I insisted. I mean, I'm twelve. So I *was* acting my age. If you can't play jokes on your parents and try to have a little fun at twelve, when *can* you?

"Don't be such a smart guy," Dad said, giving me his stern look. "There's a lot of work to be done around here, you know, Jerry. You could help out."

He shoved the broom toward me.

I raised both hands as if shielding myself from danger, and backed away. "Dad, you *know* I'm allergic!" I cried.

"Allergic to dust?" he asked.

"No. Allergic to work!"

I expected them to laugh, but they just stormed out of the room, muttering to themselves. "You can at least look after Bonkers," Mom called back to me. "Keep her out of the movers' way."

"Yeah. Sure," I called back. Bonkers is our cat, and there's *no way* I can keep Bonkers from doing anything!

Let me say right out that Bonkers is *not* my favorite member of our family. In fact, I keep as far away from Bonkers as I can.

No one ever explained to the stupid cat that she's supposed to be a pet. Instead, I think Bonkers believes she's a wild, man-eating tiger. Or maybe a vampire bat.

Her favorite trick is to climb up on the back of a chair or a high shelf — and then leap with her claws out onto your shoulders. I can't tell you how many good T-shirts have been ripped to shreds by this trick of hers. Or how much blood I've lost.

The cat is nasty — just plain vicious.

She's all black except for a white circle over her forehead and one eye. Mom and Dad think she's just wonderful. They're always picking her up, and petting her, and telling her how adorable she is. Bonkers usually scratches them and makes them bleed. But they never learn.

When we moved to this new house, I was hoping maybe Bonkers would get left behind. But, no way. Mom made sure that Bonkers was in the car first, right next to me.

And of course the stupid cat threw up in the back seat.

Whoever heard of a cat who gets carsick? She did it deliberately because she's horrible and vicious.

Anyway, I ignored Mom's request to keep an eye on her. In fact, I crept into the kitchen and opened the back door, hoping maybe Bonkers would run away and get lost.

Then I continued my exploring.

Our other house was tiny, but new. This house was old. The floorboards creaked. The windows rattled. The house seemed to groan when you walked through it.

But it was really big. I discovered all kinds of little rooms and deep closets. One upstairs closet was as big as my old bedroom!

My new bedroom was at the end of the hall on the second floor. There were three other rooms and a bathroom up there. I wondered what Mom and Dad planned to do with all those rooms.

I decided to suggest that one of them be made into a Nintendo room. We could put a wide-screen TV in there to play the games on. It would be really neat.

As I made plans for my new video game room, I started to feel a little cheered up. I mean, it isn't easy to move to a new house in a new town.

I'm not the kind of kid who cries much. But I have to admit that I felt like crying a *lot* when we moved away from Cedarville. Especially when I had to say good-bye to my friends.

Especially Sean. Sean is a great guy. Mom and

Dad don't like him too much because he's kind of noisy and he likes to burp real loud. But Sean is my best friend.

I mean he *was* my best friend.

I don't have any friends here in New Goshen.

Mom said Sean could come stay with us for a few weeks this summer. That was really nice of her, especially since she hates his burping so much.

But it didn't really cheer me up.

Exploring the new house was making me feel a little better. The room next to mine can be a gym, I decided. We'll get all those great-looking exercise machines they show on TV.

The movers were hauling stuff into my room, so I couldn't go in there. I pulled open a door to what I thought was a closet. But to my surprise, I saw a narrow, wooden stairway. I guessed it led up to an attic.

An attic!

I'd never had an attic before. I'll bet it's filled with all kinds of great old stuff, I thought excitedly. Maybe the people who used to live here left their old comic book collection up there — and it's worth millions!

I was halfway up the stairs when I heard Dad's voice behind me. "Jerry, where are you going?"

"Up," I replied. That was pretty obvious.

"You really shouldn't go up there by yourself," he warned.

"Why not? Are there ghosts up here or something?" I asked.

I could hear his heavy footsteps on the wooden stairs. He followed me up. "Hot up here," he muttered, adjusting his glasses on his nose. "It's so stuffy."

He tugged on a chain suspended from the ceiling, and an overhead light came on, casting pale yellow light down on us.

I glanced quickly around. It was all one room, long and low, the ceiling slanting down on both sides under the roof. I'm not very tall, but I reached up and touched the ceiling.

There were tiny, round windows at both ends. But they were covered with dust and didn't let in much light.

"It's empty," I muttered, very disappointed.

"We can store a lot of junk up here," Dad said, looking around.

"Hey — what's that?" I spotted something against the far wall and began walking quickly toward it. The floorboards squeaked and creaked under my sneakers.

I saw a gray, quilted cover over something large. Maybe it's some kind of treasure chest, I thought.

7

No one ever accused me of not having a good imagination.

Dad was right behind me as I grabbed the heavy cover with both hands and pulled it away.

And stared at a shiny, black piano.

"Wow," Dad murmured, scratching his bald spot, staring at the piano with surprise. "Wow. Wow. Why did they leave *this* behind?"

I shrugged. "It looks like new," I said. I hit some keys with my pointer finger. "Sounds good."

Dad hit some keys, too. "It's a really good piano," he said, rubbing his hand lightly over the keyboard. "I wonder what it's doing hidden up here in the attic like this. . . ."

"It's a mystery," I agreed.

I had no idea how big a mystery it really was.

I couldn't get to sleep that night. I mean, there was no way.

I was in my good old bed from our old house. But it was facing the wrong direction. And it was against a different wall. And the light from the neighbor's back porch was shining through the window. The window rattled from the wind. And all these creepy shadows were moving back and forth across the ceiling.

I'm *never* going to be able to sleep in this new room, I realized.

It's too different. Too creepy. Too big.

I'm going to be awake for the rest of my life!

I just lay there, eyes wide open, staring up at the weird shadows.

I had just started to relax and drift off to sleep when I heard the music.

Piano music.

At first, I thought it was coming from outside. But I quickly realized it was coming from up above me. From the attic!

I sat straight up and listened. Yes. Some kind of classical music. Right over my head.

I kicked off the covers and lowered my feet to the floor.

Who could be up in the attic playing the piano in the middle of the night? I wondered. It couldn't be Dad. He can't play a note. And the only thing Mom can play is "Chopsticks," and not very well.

Maybe it's Bonkers, I told myself.

I stood up and listened. The music continued. Very softly. But I could hear it clearly. Every note.

I started to make my way to the door and stubbed my toe against a carton that hadn't been unpacked. "Ow!" I cried out, grabbing my foot and hopping around until the pain faded.

Mom and Dad couldn't hear me, I knew. Their bedroom was downstairs.

I held my breath and listened. I could still hear the piano music above my head.

9

Walking slowly, carefully, I stepped out of my room and into the hallway. The floorboards creaked under my bare feet. The floor was cold.

I pulled open the attic door and leaned into the darkness.

The music floated down. It was sad music, very slow, very soft.

"Who — who's up there?" I stammered.

2

The sad music continued, floating down the dark, narrow stairway to me.

"Who's up there?" I repeated, my voice shaking just a little.

Again, no reply.

I leaned into the darkness, peering up toward the attic. "Mom, is that you? Dad?"

No reply. The melody was so sad, so slow.

Before I even realized what I was doing, I was climbing the stairs. They groaned loudly under my bare feet.

The air grew hot and stuffy as I reached the top of the stairs and stepped into the dark attic.

The piano music surrounded me now. The notes seemed to be coming from all directions at once.

"Who is it?" I demanded in a shrill, high-pitched

11

voice. I guess I was a little scared. "Who's up here?"

Something brushed against my face, and I nearly jumped out of my skin.

It took me a long, shuddering moment to realize it was the light chain.

I pulled it. Pale yellow light spread out over the long, narrow room.

The music stopped.

"Who's up here?" I called, squinting toward the piano against the far wall.

No one.

No one there. No one sitting at the piano.

Silence.

Except for the floorboards creaking under my feet as I walked over to the piano. I stared at it, stared at the keys.

I don't know what I expected to see. I mean, *someone* was playing the piano. *Someone* played it until the exact second the light went on. Where did they go?

I ducked down and searched under the piano.

I know it was stupid, but I wasn't thinking clearly. My heart was pounding really hard, and all kinds of crazy thoughts were spinning through my brain.

I leaned over the piano and examined the keyboard. I thought maybe this was one of those old-fashioned pianos that played by itself. A player piano. You know, like you sometimes see in cartoons.

But it looked like an ordinary piano. I didn't see anything special about it.

I sat down on the bench.

And jumped up.

The piano bench was warm! As if someone had just been sitting on it!

"Whoa!" I cried aloud, staring at the shiny, black bench.

I reached down and felt it. It was definitely warm.

But I reminded myself the whole attic was really warm, much warmer than the rest of the house. The heat seemed to float up here and stay.

I sat back down and waited for my racing heart to return to normal.

What's going on here? I asked myself, turning to stare at the piano. The black wood was polished so well, I could see the reflection of my face staring back at me.

My reflection looked pretty scared.

I lowered my eyes to the keyboard and then hit a few soft notes.

Someone had been playing this piano a few moments ago, I knew.

But how could they have vanished into thin air without me seeing them?

I plunked another note, then another. The

sound echoed through the long, empty room.

Then I heard a loud creak. From the bottom of the stairs.

I froze, my hand still on the piano keys.

Another creak. A footstep.

I stood up, surprised to find my legs all trembly.

I listened. I listened so hard, I could hear the air move.

Another footstep. Louder. Closer.

Someone was on the stairs. Someone was climbing to the attic.

Someone was coming for me.

3

Creak. Creak.

The stairs gave way beneath heavy footsteps.

My breath caught in my throat. I felt as if I would suffocate.

Frozen in front of the piano, I searched for a place to hide. But of course there wasn't any.

Creak. Creak.

And then, as I stared in terror, a head poked up above the stairwell.

"Dad!" I cried.

"Jerry, what on earth are you doing up here?" He stepped into the pale yellow light. His thinning brown hair was standing up all over his head. His pajama pants were twisted. One leg had rolled up to the knee. He squinted at me. He didn't have his glasses on.

"Dad — I — I thought — " I sputtered. I knew I sounded like a complete jerk. But give me a break — I was *scared*!

15

"Do you know what time it is?" Dad demanded angrily. He glanced down at his wrist, but he wasn't wearing his watch. "It's the middle of the night, Jerry!"

"I — I know, Dad," I said, starting to feel a little better. I walked over to him. "I heard piano music, see. And so I thought — "

"You *what*?" His dark eyes grew wide. His mouth dropped open. "You heard *what*?"

"Piano music," I repeated. "Up here. So I came upstairs to check it out, and — "

"Jerry!" Dad exploded. His face got really red. "It's too late for your dumb jokes!"

"But, Dad — " I started to protest.

"Your mother and I killed ourselves unpacking and moving furniture all day," Dad said, sighing wearily. "We're both exhausted, Jerry. I shouldn't have to tell you that I'm in no mood for jokes. I have to go to work tomorrow morning. I need some sleep."

"Sorry, Dad," I said quietly. I could see there was no way I was going to get him to believe me about the piano music.

"I know you're excited about being in a new house," Dad said, putting a hand on the shoulder of my pajama shirt. "But, come on. Back to your room. You need your sleep, too."

I glanced back at the piano. It glimmered darkly

16

in the pale yellow light. As if it were breathing. As if it were alive.

I pictured it rumbling toward me, chasing me to the stairs.

Crazy, weird thoughts. I guess I was more tired than I thought!

"Would you like to learn to play it?" Dad asked suddenly.

"Huh?" His question caught me by surprise.

"Would you like to take piano lessons? We could have the piano brought downstairs. There's room for it in the family room."

"Well . . . maybe," I replied. "Yeah. That might be neat."

He took his hand from my shoulder. Then he straightened his pajama bottoms and started down the stairs. "I'll discuss it with your mother," he said. "I'm sure she'll be pleased. She always wanted someone to be musical in the family. Pull the light chain, okay?"

Obediently, I reached up and clicked off the light. The sudden darkness was so black, it startled me. I stayed close behind my dad as we made our way down the creaking stairs.

Back in my bed, I pulled the covers up to my chin. It was kind of cold in my room. Outside, the winter wind gusted hard. The bedroom window rattled and shook, as if it were shivering.

17

Piano lessons might be fun, I thought. If they let me learn to play rock piano, not that drippy, boring classical stuff.

After a few lessons, maybe I could get a synthesizer. Get two or three different keyboards. Hook them up to a computer.

Then I could do some composing. Maybe get a group together.

Yeah. It could be really excellent.

I closed my eyes.

The window rattled again. The old house seemed to groan.

I'll get used to these noises, I told myself. I'll get used to this old house. After a few nights, I won't even hear the noises.

I had just about drifted off to sleep when I heard the soft, sad piano music begin again.

4

Monday morning, I woke up very early. My cat clock with the moving tail and eyes wasn't unpacked yet. But I could tell it was early by the pale gray light coming through my bedroom window.

I got dressed quickly, pulling on a clean pair of faded jeans and a dark green pullover shirt that wasn't too wrinkled. It was my first day at my new school, so I was pretty excited.

I spent more time on my hair than I usually do. My hair is brown and thick and wiry, and it takes me a long time to slick it down and make it lie flat the way I like it.

When I finally got it right, I made my way down the hall to the front stairs. The house was still silent and dark.

I stopped outside the attic door. It was wide open.

Hadn't I closed it when I'd come downstairs with my dad?

Yes. I remembered shutting it tight. And now, here it was, wide open.

I felt a cold chill on the back on my neck. I closed the door, listening for the click.

Jerry, take it easy, I warned myself. Maybe the latch is loose. Maybe the attic door always swings open. It's an old house, remember?

I'd been thinking about the piano music. Maybe it was the wind blowing through the piano strings, I told myself.

Maybe there was a hole or something in the attic window. And the wind blew in and made it sound as if the piano were playing.

I wanted to believe it had been the wind that made that slow, sad music. I wanted to believe it, so I did.

I checked the attic door one more time, making sure it was latched, then headed down to the kitchen.

Mom and Dad were still in their room. I could hear them getting dressed.

The kitchen was dark and a little cold. I wanted to turn up the furnace, but I didn't know where the thermostat was.

Not all of our kitchen stuff had been unpacked. Cartons were still stacked against the wall, filled with glasses and plates and stuff.

I heard someone coming down the hall.

A big, empty carton beside the refrigerator gave me an idea. Snickering to myself, I jumped inside it and pulled the lid over me.

I held my breath and waited.

Footsteps in the kitchen. I couldn't tell if it was Mom or Dad.

My heart was pounding. I continued to hold my breath. If I didn't, I knew I would burst out laughing.

The footsteps went right past my carton to the sink. I heard water running. Whoever it was filled the kettle.

Footsteps to the stove.

I couldn't wait anymore.

"SURPRISE!" I screamed and jumped to my feet in the carton.

Dad let out a startled shriek and dropped the kettle. It landed on his foot with a *thud*, then tilted onto its side on the floor.

Water puddled around Dad's feet. The kettle rolled toward the stove. Dad was howling and holding his injured foot and hopping up and down.

I was laughing like a maniac! You should've seen the look on Dad's face when I jumped up from the carton. I really thought he was going to drop his teeth!

Mom came bursting into the room, still buttoning her sleeve cuffs. "What's going on in here?" she cried.

"Just Jerry and his stupid jokes," Dad grumbled.

"Jerome!" Mom shouted, seeing all the spilled water on the linoleum. "Give us a break."

"Just trying to help wake you up," I said, grinning. They complain a lot, but they're used to my twisted sense of humor.

I heard the piano music again that night.

It was definitely not the wind. I recognized the same sad melody.

I listened for a few moments. It came from right above my room.

Who's up there? Who can be playing? I asked myself.

I started to climb out of bed and investigate. But it was cold in my room, and I was really tired from my first day at the new school.

So I pulled the covers over my head to drown out the piano music, and quickly fell asleep.

"Did you hear the piano music last night?" I asked my mom.

"Eat your cornflakes," she replied. She tightened the belt of her bathrobe and leaned toward me over the kitchen table.

"How come I have to have cornflakes?" I grumbled, mushing the spoon around in the bowl.

"You know the rules," she said, frowning. "Junk cereal only on weekends."

"Stupid rule," I muttered. "I think cornflakes is a junk cereal."

"Don't give me a hard time," Mom complained, rubbing her temples. "I have a headache this morning."

"From the piano playing last night?" I asked.

"What piano playing?" she demanded irritably. "Why do you keep talking about piano playing?"

"Didn't you hear it? The piano in the attic? Someone was playing it last night."

She jumped to her feet. "Oh, Jerry, please. No jokes this morning, okay? I told you I have a headache."

"Did I hear you talking about the piano?" Dad came into the kitchen, carrying the morning newspaper. "The guys are coming this afternoon to carry it down to the family room." He smiled at me. "Limber up those fingers, Jerry."

Mom had walked over to the counter to pour herself a cup of coffee. "Are you really interested in this piano?" she demanded, eyeing me skeptically. "Are you really going to practice and work at it?"

"Of course," I replied. "Maybe."

The two piano movers were there when I got home from school. They weren't very big, but they were strong.

I went up to the attic and watched them while Mom pulled cartons out of the family room to make a place for it.

The two men used ropes and a special kind of dolly. They tilted the piano onto its side, then hoisted it onto the dolly.

Lowering it down the narrow staircase was really hard. It bumped against the wall several times, even though they moved slowly and carefully.

Both movers were really red-faced and sweaty by the time they got the piano downstairs. I followed them as they rolled it across the living room, then through the dining room.

Mom came out of the kitchen, her hands jammed into her jeans pockets, and watched from the doorway as they rolled the dolly with the piano into the family room.

The men strained to tilt it right side up. The black, polished wood really glowed in the bright afternoon sunlight through the family room windows.

Then, as they started to lower the piano to the floor, Mom opened her mouth and started to scream.

5

"The cat! The cat!" Mom shrieked, her face all twisted in alarm.

Sure enough, Bonkers was standing right in the spot where they were lowering the piano.

The piano thudded heavily to the floor. Bonkers ran out from under it just in time.

Too bad! I thought, shaking my head. That dumb cat almost got what it deserved.

The men were apologizing as they tried to catch their breath, mopping their foreheads with their red-and-white bandannas.

Mom ran to Bonkers and picked her up. "My poor little kitty."

Of course Bonkers swiped at Mom's arm, her claws tearing out several threads in the sweater sleeve. Mom dropped her to the floor, and the creature slithered quickly out of the room.

"She's a little freaked out being in a new house," Mom told the two workers.

"She *always* acts like that," I told them.

A few minutes later, the movers were gone. Mom was in her room, trying to fix her sweater. And I was alone in the family room with my piano.

I sat on the bench and slid back and forth on it. The bench was polished and smooth. It was real slippery.

I planned a really funny comedy act where I sit down to play the piano for Mom and Dad, only the bench is so slippery, I keep sliding right onto the floor.

I practiced sliding and falling for a while. I was having fun.

Falling is one of my hobbies. It isn't as easy as it looks.

After a while, I got tired of falling. I just sat on the bench and stared at the keys. I tried picking out a song, hitting notes until I found the right ones.

I started to get excited about learning to play the piano.

I imagined it was going to be fun.

I was wrong. Very wrong.

Saturday afternoon, I stood staring out the living room window. It was a blustery, gray day. It looked like it was about to snow.

I saw the piano teacher walking up the driveway. He was right on time. Two o'clock.

Pressing my face against the window, I could see that he was big, kind of fat. He wore a long, puffy red coat and he had bushy white hair. From this distance, he sort of looked like Santa Claus.

He walked very stiffly, as if his knees weren't good. Arthritis or something, I guessed.

Dad had found his name in a tiny ad in the back of the New Goshen newspaper. He showed it to me. It said:

THE SHREEK SCHOOL
New Method Piano Training

Since it was the only ad in the paper for a piano teacher, Dad called it.

And now, Mom and Dad were greeting the teacher at the door and taking his heavy red coat. "Jerry, this is Dr. Shreek," Dad said, motioning for me to leave my place by the window.

Dr. Shreek smiled at me. "Hello, Jerry."

He really did look like Santa Claus, except he had a white mustache, no beard. He had round, red cheeks and a friendly smile, and his blue eyes sort of twinkled as he greeted me.

He wore a white shirt that was coming untucked around his big belly, and baggy, gray pants.

I stepped forward and shook hands with him. His hand was red and kind of spongy. "Nice to meet you, Dr. Shreek," I said politely.

Mom and Dad grinned at each other. They could never believe it when I was polite!

Dr. Shreek put his spongy hand on my shoulder. "I know I have a funny name," he said, chuckling. "I probably should change it. But, you have to admit, it's a real attention-getter!"

We all laughed.

Dr. Shreek's expression turned serious. "Have you ever played an instrument before, Jerry?"

I thought hard. "Well, I had a kazoo once!"

Everyone laughed again.

"The piano is a little more difficult than the kazoo," Dr. Shreek said, still chuckling. "Let me see your piano."

I led him through the dining room and into the family room. He walked stiffly, but it didn't seem to slow him down.

Mom and Dad excused themselves and disappeared upstairs to do more unpacking.

Dr. Shreek studied the piano keys. Then he lifted the back and examined the strings with his eyes. "Very fine instrument," he murmured. "Very fine."

"We found it here," I told him.

His mouth opened in a little O of surprise. "You found it?"

"In the attic. Someone just left it up there," I said.

"How strange," he replied, rubbing his pudgy

chin. He straightened his white mustache as he stared at the keys. "Don't you wonder who played this piano before you?" he asked softly. "Don't you wonder whose fingers touched these keys?"

"Well . . ." I really didn't know what to say.

"What a mystery," he said in a whisper. Then he motioned for me to take a seat on the piano bench.

I was tempted to do my comedy act and slide right off onto the floor. But I decided I'd save it for when I knew him better.

He seemed like a nice, jolly kind of guy. But I didn't want him to think I wasn't serious about learning to play.

He dropped down beside me on the bench. He was so wide, there was barely room for the two of us.

"Will you be giving me lessons here at home every week?" I asked, scooting over as far as I could to make room.

"I'll give you lessons at home at first," he replied, his blue eyes twinkling at me. "Then, if you show promise, Jerry, you can come to my school."

I started to say something, but he grabbed my hands.

"Let me take a look," he said, raising my hands close to his face. He turned them over and studied both sides. Then he carefully examined my fingers.

"What beautiful hands!" he exclaimed breath-lessly. "Excellent hands!"

I stared down at my hands. They didn't look like anything special to me. Just normal hands.

"Excellent hands," Dr. Shreek repeated. He placed them carefully on the piano keys. He showed me what each note was, starting with C, and he had me play each one with the correct finger.

"Next week we will start," he told me, climbing up from the piano bench. "I just wanted to meet you today."

He searched through a small bag he had leaned against the wall. He pulled out a workbook and handed it to me. It was called *Beginning to Play: A Hands-On Approach.*

"Look this over, Jerry. Try to learn the notes on pages two and three." He made his way over to his coat, which Dad had draped over the back of the couch.

"See you next Saturday," I said. I felt a little disappointed that the lesson had been so short. I thought I'd be playing some great rock riffs by now.

He pulled on his coat, then came back to where I was sitting. "I think you will be an excellent student, Jerry," he said, smiling.

I muttered thanks. I was surprised to see that

his eyes had settled on my hands. "Excellent. Excellent," he whispered.

I felt a sudden chill.

I think it was the hungry expression on his face.

What's so special about my hands? I wondered. *Why does he like them so much?*

It was weird. Definitely weird.

But of course I didn't know *how* weird. . . .

6

CDEFGABC.

I practiced the notes on pages two and three of the piano workbook. The book showed which finger to use and everything.

This is easy, I thought.

So when can I start playing some rock and roll?

I was still picking out notes when Mom surfaced from the basement and poked her head into the family room. Her hair had come loose from the bandanna she had tied around her head, and she had dirt smudges on her forehead.

"Did Dr. Shreek leave already?" she asked, surprised.

"Yeah. He said he just wanted to meet me," I told her. "He's coming back next Saturday. He said I had excellent hands."

"You do?" She brushed the hair out of her eyes. "Well, maybe you can take those excellent hands down to the basement and use them to help us unpack some boxes."

"Oh, no!" I cried, and I slid off the piano bench and fell to the floor.

She didn't laugh.

That night, I heard piano music.

I sat straight up in bed and listened. The music floated up from downstairs.

I climbed out of bed. The floorboards were cold under my bare feet. I was supposed to have a carpet, but Dad hadn't had time to put it down yet.

The house was silent. Through my bedroom window, I could see a gentle snow coming down, tiny, fine flakes, gray against the black sky.

"Someone is playing the piano," I said aloud, startled by the huskiness of my sleep-filled voice.

"Someone is downstairs playing my piano."

Mom and Dad must hear it, I thought. Their room is at the far end of the house. But they are downstairs. They must hear it.

I crept to my bedroom door.

The same slow, sad melody. I had been humming it just before dinner. Mom had asked me where I'd heard it, and I couldn't remember.

I leaned against the doorframe, my heart pounding, and listened. The music drifted up so clearly, I could hear each note.

Who is playing?

Who?

I had to find out. Trailing my hand along the wall, I hurried through the dark hallway. There was a night-light by the stairway, but I was always forgetting to turn it on.

I made my way to the stairs. Then, gripping the wooden banister tightly, I crept down, one step at a time, trying to be silent.

Trying not to scare the piano player away.

The wooden stairs creaked quietly under my weight. But the music continued. Soft and sad, almost mournful.

Tiptoeing and holding my breath, I crossed the living room. A streetlight cast a wash of pale yellow across the floor. Through the large front window, I could see the tiny snowflakes drifting down.

I nearly tripped over an unpacked carton of vases left next to the coffee table. But I grabbed the back of the couch and kept myself from falling.

The music stopped. Then started again.

I leaned against the couch, waiting for my heart to stop pounding so hard.

Where are Mom and Dad? I wondered, staring toward the back hallway where their room was.

Can't they hear the piano, too? Aren't they curious? Don't they wonder who is in the family room in the middle of the night, playing such a sad song?

I took a deep breath and pushed myself away from the couch. Slowly, silently, I made my way through the dining room.

It was darker back there. No light from the street. I moved carefully, aware of all the chairs and table legs that could trip me up.

The door to the family room stood just a few feet ahead of me. The music grew louder.

I took a step. Then another.

I moved into the open doorway.

Who is it? Who is it?

I peered into the darkness.

But before I could see, someone uttered a horrifying shriek behind me — and shoved me hard, pushing me down to the floor.

7

I hit the floor hard on my knees and elbows.

Another loud shriek — right in my ears.

My shoulders throbbed with pain.

The lights came on.

"Bonkers!" I roared.

The cat leapt off my shoulders and scurried out of the room.

"Jerry — what are you doing? What's going on?" Mom demanded angrily as she ran into the room.

"What's all the racket?" Dad was right behind her, squinting hard without his glasses.

"Bonkers jumped on me!" I screamed, still on the floor. "Ow. My shoulder. That stupid cat!"

"But, Jerry — " Mom started. She bent to help pull me up.

"That stupid cat!" I fumed. "She jumped down from that shelf. She scared me to death. And look — look at my pajama shirt!"

The cat's claws had ripped right through the shoulder.

"Are you cut? Are you bleeding?" Mom asked, pulling the shirt collar down to examine my shoulder.

"We really have to do something about that cat," Dad muttered. "Jerry is right. She's a menace."

Mom immediately jumped to Bonkers' defense. "She was just frightened, that's all. She probably thought Jerry was a burglar."

"A burglar?" I shrieked in a voice so high, only dogs could hear me. "How could she think I was a burglar? Aren't cats supposed to see in the dark?"

"Well, what were you doing down here, Jerry?" Mom asked, straightening my pajama shirt collar. She patted my shoulder. As if that would help.

"Yeah. Why were you skulking around down here?" Dad demanded, squinting hard at me. He could barely see a thing without his glasses.

"I wasn't skulking around," I replied angrily. "I heard piano music and — "

"You *what*?" Mom interrupted.

"I heard piano music. In the family room. So I came down to see who was playing."

My parents were both staring at me as if I were a Martian.

"Didn't you hear it?" I cried.

They shook their heads.

I turned to the piano. No one there. Of course.

I hurried over to the piano bench, leaned down, and rubbed my hand over the surface.

It was warm.

"Someone was sitting here. I can tell!" I exclaimed.

"Not funny," Mom said, making a face.

"Not funny, Jerry," Dad echoed. "You came down here to pull some kind of joke — didn't you!" he accused.

"Huh? Me?"

"Don't play innocent, Jerome," Mom said, rolling her eyes. "We know you. You're *never* innocent."

"I wasn't playing a joke!" I cried angrily. "I heard music, someone playing — "

"Who?" Dad demanded. "Who was playing?"

"Maybe it was Bonkers," Mom joked.

Dad laughed, but I didn't.

"What was the joke, Jerry? What were you planning to do?" Dad asked.

"Were you going to do something to the piano?" Mom demanded, staring at me so hard, I could practically *feel* it. "That's a valuable instrument, you know."

I sighed wearily. I felt so frustrated, I wanted to shout, scream, throw a fit, and maybe slug them both. "The piano is *haunted*!" I shouted. The words just popped into my head.

"Huh?" It was Dad's turn to give me a hard stare.

"It must be haunted!" I insisted, my voice shaking. "It keeps playing — but there's no one playing it!"

"I've heard enough," Mom muttered, shaking her head. "I'm going back to bed."

"Ghosts, huh?" Dad asked, rubbing his chin thoughtfully. He stepped up to me and lowered his head, the way he does when he's about to unload something serious. "Listen, Jerry, I know this house might seem old and kind of scary. And I know how hard it was for you to leave your friends behind and move away."

"Dad, please — " I interrupted.

But he kept going. "The house is just old, Jerry. Old and a little rundown. But that doesn't mean it's haunted. These ghosts of yours — don't you see? — they're really your fears coming out."

Dad was a psychology major in college.

"Skip the lecture, Dad," I told him. "I'm going to bed."

"Okay, Jer," he said, patting my shoulder. "Remember — in a few weeks, you'll know I'm right. In a few weeks, this ghost business will all seem silly to you."

Boy, was he wrong!

I slammed my locker shut and started to pull on my jacket. The long school hallway echoed with laughing voices, slamming lockers, calls and shouts.

The halls were always noisier on Friday afternoons. School was over, and the weekend was here!

"Oooh, what's that smell?" I cried, making a disgusted face.

Beside me, a girl was down on her knees, pawing through a pile of junk on the floor of her locker. "I *wondered* where that apple disappeared to!" she exclaimed.

She climbed to her feet, holding a shriveled, brown apple in one hand. The sour aroma invaded my nostrils. I thought I was going to hurl!

I must have been making a funny face, because she burst out laughing. "Hungry?" She pushed the disgusting thing in my face.

"No thanks." I pushed it back toward her. "You can have it."

She laughed again. She was kind of pretty. She had long, straight black hair and green eyes.

She set the rotten apple down on the floor. "You're the new kid, right?" she asked. "I'm Kim. Kim Li Chin."

"Hi," I said. I told her my name. "You're in my

math class. And science class," I told her.

She turned back to her locker, searching for more stuff. "I know," she replied. "I saw you fall out of your chair when Ms. Klein called on you."

"I just did that to be funny," I explained quickly. "I didn't really fall."

"I know," she said. She pulled a heavy gray wool sweater down over her lighter sweater. Then she reached down and removed a black violin case from her locker.

"Is that your lunchbox?" I joked.

"I'm late for my violin lesson," she answered, slamming her locker shut. She struggled to push the padlock closed.

"I'm taking piano lessons," I told her. "Well, I mean I just started."

"You know, I live across the street from you," she said, adjusting her backpack over her shoulder. "I watched you move in."

"Really?" I replied, surprised. "Well, maybe you could come over and we could play together. I mean, play music. You know. I'm taking lessons every Saturday with Dr. Shreek."

Her mouth dropped open in horror as she stared at me. "You're doing *what*?" she cried.

"Taking piano lessons with Dr. Shreek," I repeated.

"Oh!" She uttered a soft cry, spun around, and began running toward the front door.

"Hey, Kim — " I called after her. "Kim — what's wrong?"

But she disappeared out the door.

8

"Excellent hands. Excellent!" Dr. Shreek declared.

"Thanks," I replied awkwardly.

I was seated at the piano bench, hunched over the piano, my hands spread over the keys. Dr. Shreek stood beside me, staring down at my hands.

"Now play the piece again," he instructed, raising his blue eyes to mine. His smile faded beneath his white mustache as his expression turned serious. "Play it carefully, my boy. Slowly and carefully. Concentrate on your fingers. Each finger is alive, remember — *alive!*"

"My fingers are alive," I repeated, staring down at them.

What a weird thought, I told myself.

I began to play, concentrating on the notes on the music sheet propped above the keyboard. It was a simple melody, a beginner's piece by Bach.

I thought it sounded pretty good.

"The fingers! The fingers!" Dr. Shreek cried. He leaned down toward the keyboard, bringing his face close to mine. "Remember, the fingers are alive!"

What's with this guy and fingers? I asked myself.

I finished the piece. I glanced up to see a frown darken his face.

"Pretty good, Jerry," he said softly. "Now let us try it a bit faster."

"I goofed up the middle part," I confessed.

"You lost your concentration," he replied. He reached down and spread my fingers over the keys. "Again," he instructed. "But faster. And concentrate. Concentrate on your hands."

I took a deep breath and began the piece again. But this time I messed it up immediately.

I started over. It sounded pretty good. Only a few clunkers.

I wondered if Mom and Dad could hear it. Then I remembered they had gone grocery shopping.

Dr. Shreek and I were alone in the house.

I finished the piece and lowered my hands to my lap with a sigh.

"Not bad. Now faster," Dr. Shreek ordered.

"Maybe we should try another piece," I suggested. "This is getting kind of boring."

"Faster this time," he replied, totally ignoring

me. "The hands, Jerry. Remember the hands. They're alive. Let them breathe!"

Let them breathe?

I stared down at my hands, expecting them to talk back to me!

"Begin," Dr. Shreek instructed sternly, leaning over me. "Faster."

Sighing, I began to play again. The same boring tune.

"Faster!" the instructor cried. "Faster, Jerry!"

I played faster. My fingers moved over the keys, pounding them hard. I tried to concentrate on the notes, but I was playing too fast for my eyes to keep up.

"Faster!" Dr. Shreek cried excitedly, staring down at the keyboard. "That's it! Faster, Jerry!"

My fingers were moving so fast, they were a blur!

"Faster! Faster!"

Was I playing the right notes? I couldn't tell. It was too fast, too fast to *hear*!

"Faster, Jerry!" Dr. Shreek instructed, screaming at the top of his lungs. "Faster! The hands are alive! Alive!"

"I can't do it!" I cried. "Please — !"

"Faster! Faster!"

"I can't!" I insisted. It was too fast. Too fast to play. Too fast to hear.

I tried to stop.

But my hands kept going!

"Stop! Stop!" I screamed down at them in horror.

"Faster! Play faster!" Dr. Shreek ordered, his eyes wide with excitement, his face bright red. "The hands are *alive!*"

"No — please! Stop!" I called down to my hands. "Stop playing!"

But they really *were* alive. They wouldn't stop.

My fingers flew over the keys. A crazy tidal wave of notes flooded the family room.

"Faster! Faster!" the instructor ordered.

And despite my frightened cries to stop, my hands gleefully obeyed him, playing on, faster and faster and faster.

9

Faster and faster, the music swirled around me.

It's choking me, I thought, gasping for breath. I can't breathe.

I struggled to stop my hands. But they moved frantically over the keyboard, playing louder. Louder.

My hands began to ache. They throbbed with pain.

But still they played. Faster. Louder.

Until I woke up.

I sat up in bed, wide awake.

And realized I was sitting on my hands.

They both tingled painfully. Pins and needles. My hands had fallen asleep.

I had been asleep. The weird piano lesson — it was a dream.

A strange nightmare.

"It's still Friday night," I said aloud. The sound of my voice helped bring me out of the dream.

47

I shook my hands, trying to get the circulation going, trying to stop the uncomfortable tingling.

My forehead was sweating, a cold sweat. My entire body felt clammy. The pajama shirt stuck damply to my back. I shuddered, suddenly chilled.

And realized the piano music hadn't stopped.

I gasped and gripped the bedcovers tightly. Holding my breath, I listened.

The notes floated into my dark bedroom.

Not the frantic roar of notes from my dream. The slow, sad melody I had heard before.

Still trembling from my frightening dream, I climbed silently out of bed.

The music floated up from the family room, so soft, so mournful.

Who is playing down there?

My hands still tingled as I made my way over the cold floorboards to the doorway. I stopped in the hall and listened.

The tune ended, then began again.

Tonight I am going to solve this mystery, I told myself.

My heart was pounding. My entire body was tingling now. Pins and needles up and down my back.

Ignoring how frightened I felt, I walked quickly down the hall to the stairway. The dim night-light down near the floor made my shadow rise up on the wall.

It startled me for a moment. I hung back. But then I hurried down the stairs, leaning hard on the banister to keep the steps from creaking.

The piano music grew louder as I crossed the dark living room.

Nothing is going to stop me tonight, I told myself. Nothing.

Tonight I am going to see who is playing the piano.

The music continued, soft high notes, so light and sad.

I tiptoed carefully through the dining room, holding my breath, listening to the music.

I stepped up to the doorway to the family room.

The music continued, a little louder.

The same melody, over and over.

Peering into the darkness, I stepped into the room.

One step. Another.

The piano was only a few feet in front of me.

The music was so clear, so close.

But I couldn't see anyone on the piano bench. I couldn't see anyone there at all.

Who is playing? Who is playing this sad, sad music in the darkness?

Trembling all over, I took another step closer. Another step.

"Who — who's there?" I called out in a choked whisper.

I stopped, my hands knotted tensely into tight fists at my sides. I stared hard into the blackness, straining to see.

The music continued. I could hear fingers on the keys, hear the slide of feet on the pedals.

"Who's there? Who's playing?" My voice was tiny and shrill.

There's *no one* here, I realized to my horror.

The piano is playing, but there's *no one* here.

Then, slowly, very slowly, like a gray cloud forming in the night sky, the ghost began to appear.

10

At first I could just see faint outlines, pale lines of gray moving against the blackness.

I gasped. My heart was pounding so hard, I thought it would burst.

The gray lines took shape, began to fill in.

I stood frozen in terror, too frightened to run or even look away.

And as I stared, a woman came into view. I couldn't tell if she was young or old. She had her head down and her eyes closed, and was concentrating on the piano keys.

She had long, wavy hair hanging loose down to her shoulders. She wore a short-sleeved top and a long skirt. Her face, her skin, her hair — all gray. Everything was gray.

She continued to play as if I weren't standing there.

Her eyes were closed. Her lips formed a sad smile.

She was kind of pretty, I realized.

But she was a ghost. A ghost playing the piano in our family room.

"Who are you? What are you doing here?" My high-pitched, tight voice startled me. The words came flying out, almost beyond my control.

She stopped playing and opened her eyes. She stared hard at me, studying me. Her smile faded quickly. Her face revealed no emotion at all.

I stared back, into the gray. It was like looking at someone in a heavy, dark fog.

With the music stopped, the house had become so quiet, so terrifyingly quiet. "Who — who are you?" I repeated, stammering in my tiny voice.

Her gray eyes narrowed in sadness. "This is my house," she said. Her voice was a dry whisper, as dry as dead leaves. As dry as death.

"This is my house." The whispered words seemed to come from far away, so soft I wasn't sure I had heard them.

"I — don't understand," I choked out, feeling a cold chill at the back of my neck. "What are you doing here?"

"My house," came the whispered reply. "My piano."

"But who *are* you?" I repeated. "Are you a *ghost*?"

As I uttered my frightened question, she let out

a loud sigh. And as I stared into the grayness, I saw her face begin to change.

The eyes closed, and her cheeks began to droop. Her gray skin appeared to fall, to melt away. It drooped like cookie batter, like soft clay. It fell onto her shoulders, then tumbled to the floor. Her hair followed, falling off in thick clumps.

A silent cry escaped my lips as her skull was revealed. Her gray skull.

Nothing remained of her face except for her eyes, her gray eyes, which bulged in the open sockets, staring at me through the darkness.

"Stay away from my piano!" she rasped. *"I'm warning you — STAY AWAY!"*

I backed up and turned away from the hideous, rasping skull. I tried to scramble away, but my legs didn't cooperate.

I fell.

Hit the floor on my knees.

I struggled to pull myself up, but I was shaking too hard.

"Stay away from my piano!" The gray skull glared at me with its bulging eyes.

"Mom! Dad!" I tried to scream, but it came out a muffled whisper.

I scrambled to my feet, my heart pounding, my throat closed tight with fear.

"This is my house! My piano! STAY AWAY!"

"Mom! Help me! Dad!"

This time I managed to call out. "Mom — Dad — please!"

To my relief, I heard bumping and clumping in the hall. Heavy footsteps.

"Jerry? Jerry? Where are you?" Mom called. "Ow!" I heard her bump into something in the dining room.

Dad reached the family room first.

I grabbed him by the shoulders, then pointed. "Dad — look! A ghost! It's a GHOST!"

11

Dad clicked on the light. Mom stumbled into the room, holding one knee.

I pointed in horror to the piano bench.

Which was now empty.

"The ghost — I saw her!" I cried, shaking all over. I turned to my parents. "Did you hear her? *Did* you?"

"Jerry, calm down." Dad put his hands on my trembling shoulders. "Calm down. It's okay. Everything is okay."

"But did you see her?" I demanded. "She was sitting there, playing the piano, and — "

"Ow. I really hurt my knee," Mom groaned. "I bumped it on the coffee table. Oww."

"Her skin dropped off. Her eyes bulged out of her skull!" I told them. I couldn't get that grinning skull out of my mind. I could still see her, as if her picture had been burned into my eyes.

"There's no one there," Dad said softly, holding onto my shoulders. "See? No one."

"Did you have a nightmare?" Mom asked, bending to massage her knee.

"It *wasn't* a nightmare!" I screamed. "I *saw* her! I really did! She *talked* to me. She told me this was her piano, her house."

"Let's sit down and talk about this," Mom suggested. "Would you like a cup of hot cocoa?"

"You don't believe me — *do* you?" I cried angrily. "I'm telling you the *truth*!"

"We don't really believe in ghosts," Dad said quietly. He guided me to the red leather couch against the wall and sat down beside me. Yawning, Mom followed us, lowering herself onto the soft couch arm.

"You don't believe in ghosts, do you, Jerry?" Mom asked.

"I do now!" I exclaimed. "Why don't you listen to me? I *heard* her playing the piano. I came downstairs and I saw her. She was a woman. She was all gray. And her face fell off. And her skull showed through. And — and — "

I saw Mom give Dad a look.

Why wouldn't they believe me?

"A woman at work was telling me about a doctor," Mom said softly, reaching down and taking my hand. "A nice doctor who talks with young people. Dr. Frye, I think his name was."

"Huh? You mean a psychiatrist?" I cried shrilly. "You think I'm *crazy*?"

"No, of course not," Mom replied quickly, still holding on to my hand. "I think something has made you very nervous, Jerry. And I don't think it would hurt to talk to someone about it."

"What are you nervous about, Jer?" Dad asked, straightening the collar of his pajama shirt. "Is it the new house? Going to a new school?"

"Is it the piano lessons?" Mom asked. "Are you worried about the lessons?" She glanced at the piano, gleaming black and shiny under the ceiling light.

"No. I'm not worried about the lessons," I muttered unhappily. "I *told* you — I'm worried about the *ghost*!"

"I'm going to make you an appointment with Dr. Frye," Mom said quietly. "Tell him about the ghost, Jerry. I'll bet he can explain it all better than your father and I can."

"I'm not crazy," I muttered.

"Something has you upset. Something is giving you bad dreams," Dad said. "This doctor will be able to explain it to you." He yawned and stood up, stretching his arms above his head. "I've got to get some sleep."

"Me, too," Mom said, letting go of my hand and climbing off the arm of the couch. "Do you think you can go to sleep now, Jerry?"

I shook my head and muttered, "I don't know."

"Do you want us to walk you to your room?" she asked.

"I'm not a little baby!" I shouted. I felt angry and frustrated. I wanted to scream and scream until they believed me.

"Well, good night, Jer," Dad said. "Tomorrow's Saturday, so you can sleep late."

"Yeah. Sure," I muttered.

"If you have any more bad dreams, wake us up," Mom said.

Dad clicked off the light. They headed down the hall to their room.

I made my way across the living room to the front stairs.

I was so angry, I wanted to hit something or kick something. I was really insulted, too.

But as I climbed the creaking stairs in the darkness, my anger turned to fear.

The ghost had vanished from the family room. What if she was waiting for me up in my room?

What if I walked into my room and the disgusting gray skull with the bulging eyeballs was staring at me from my bed?

The floorboards squeaked and groaned beneath me as I slowly made my way through the hall to my room. I suddenly felt cold all over. My throat tightened. I struggled to breathe.

She's in there. She's in there waiting for me.

I knew it. I knew she'd be there.

And if I scream, if I cry for help, Mom and Dad will just think I'm crazy.

What does the ghost want?

Why does she play the piano every night? Why did she try to frighten me? Why did she tell me to stay away?

The questions rolled through my mind. I couldn't answer them. I was too tired, too frightened to think clearly.

I hesitated outside my room, breathing hard.

Then, holding onto the wall, I gathered my courage and stepped inside.

As I moved into the darkness, the ghost rose up in front of my bed.

12

I uttered a choked cry and staggered back into the doorway.

Then I realized I was staring at my covers. I must have kicked them over the foot of the bed during my nightmare about Dr. Shreek. They stood in a clump on the floor.

My heart pounding, I crept back into the room, grabbed the blanket and sheet, and pulled them back onto the bed.

Maybe I *am* cracking up! I thought.

No way, I assured myself. I might be scared and frustrated and angry — but I saw what I saw.

Shivering, I slid into bed and pulled the covers up to my chin. I closed my eyes and tried to force the picture of the ugly gray skull from my mind.

When I finally started to drift off to sleep, I heard the piano music start again.

* * *

Dr. Shreek arrived promptly at two the next afternoon. Mom and Dad were out in the garage, unpacking more cartons. I took Dr. Shreek's coat, then led him into the family room.

It was a cold, blustery day outside, threatening snow. Dr. Shreek's cheeks were pink from the cold. With his white hair and mustache, and round belly under his baggy, white shirt, he looked more like Santa Claus than ever.

He rubbed his pudgy hands together to warm them and motioned for me to take a seat at the piano bench. "Such a beautiful instrument," he said cheerily, running a hand over the shiny, black top of the piano. "You are a very lucky young man to find this waiting for you."

"I guess," I replied without enthusiasm.

I had slept till eleven, but I was still tired. And I couldn't shake the ghost and her warning from my mind.

"Have you practiced your notes?" Dr. Shreek asked, leaning against the piano, turning the pages of the music workbook.

"A little," I told him.

"Let me see what you have learned. Here." He began to place my fingers over the keys. "Remember? This is where you start."

I played a scale.

"Excellent hands," Dr. Shreek said, smiling. "Keep repeating it, please."

The lesson went well. He kept telling me how good I was, even though I was just playing notes and a simple scale.

Maybe I *do* have some talent, I thought.

I asked him when I could begin learning some rock riffs.

He chuckled for some reason. "In due time," he replied, staring at my hands.

I heard Mom and Dad come in through the kitchen door. A few seconds later, Mom appeared in the family room, rubbing the arms of her sweater. "It's really getting cold out there," she said, smiling at Dr. Shreek. "I think it's going to snow."

"It's nice and warm in here," he replied, returning her smile.

"How's the lesson going?" Mom asked him.

"Very well," Dr. Shreek told her, winking at me. "I think Jerry shows a lot of promise. I would like him to start taking his lessons at my school."

"That's wonderful!" Mom exclaimed. "Do you really think he has talent?"

"He has excellent hands," Dr. Shreek replied.

Something about the way he said it gave me a cold chill.

"Do you teach rock music at your school?" I asked.

He patted my shoulder. "We teach all kinds of music. My school is very large, and we have many fine instructors. We have students of all ages there. Do you think you could come after school on Fridays?"

"That would be fine," Mom said.

Dr. Shreek crossed the room and handed my mom a card. "Here is the address of my school. I'm afraid it is on the other end of town."

"No problem," Mom said, studying the card. "I get off work early on Fridays. I can drive him."

"That will end our lesson for today, Jerry," Dr. Shreek said. "Practice the new notes. And I'll see you Friday."

He followed my mom to the living room. I heard them chatting quietly, but I couldn't make out what they were saying.

I stood up and walked to the window. It had started to snow, very large flakes coming down really hard. The snow was already starting to stick.

Staring into the back yard, I wondered if there were any good hills to sled on in New Goshen. And I wondered if my sled had been unpacked.

I cried out when the piano suddenly started to play.

Loud, jangling noise. Like someone pounding furiously on the keys with heavy fists.

Pound. Pound. Pound.

"Jerry — stop it!" Mom shouted from the living room.

"I'm not doing it!" I cried.

13

Dr. Frye's office wasn't the way I pictured a psychiatrist's office. It was small and bright. The walls were yellow, and there were colorful pictures of parrots and toucans and other birds hanging all around.

He didn't have a black leather couch like psychiatrists always have on TV and in the movies. Instead, he had two soft-looking, green armchairs. He didn't even have a desk. Just the two chairs.

I sat in one, and he sat in the other.

He was a lot younger than I thought he'd be. He looked younger than my dad. He had wavy red hair, slicked down with some kind of gel or something, I think. And he had a face full of freckles.

He just didn't look like a psychiatrist at all.

"Tell me about your new house," he said. He

had his legs crossed. He rested his long notepad on them as he studied me.

"It's a big, old house," I told him. "That's about it."

He asked me to describe my room, so I did.

Then we talked about the house we moved from and my old room. Then we talked about my friends back home. Then we talked about my new school.

I felt nervous when we started. But he seemed okay. He listened carefully to everything I said. And he didn't give me funny looks, like I was crazy or something.

Even when I told him about the ghost.

He scribbled down a few notes when I told him about the piano playing late at night. He stopped writing when I told him how I'd seen the ghost, and how her hair fell off and then her face, and how she had screamed at me to stay away.

"My parents didn't believe me," I said, squeezing the soft arms of the chair. My hands were sweating.

"It's a pretty weird story," Dr. Frye replied. "If you were your mom or dad, and your kid told you that story, would *you* believe it?"

"Sure," I said. "If it was true."

He chewed on his pencil eraser and stared at me.

"Do you think I'm crazy?" I asked.

He lowered his notepad. He didn't smile at the question. "No. I don't think you're crazy, Jerry. But the human mind can be really strange sometimes."

Then he launched into this long lecture about how sometimes we're afraid of something, but we don't admit to ourselves that we're afraid. So our mind does all kinds of things to show that we're afraid, even though we keep telling ourselves that we're *not* afraid.

In other words, he didn't believe me, either.

"Moving to a new house creates all kinds of stress," he said. "It is possible to start imagining that we see things, that we hear things — just so we don't admit to ourselves what we're *really* afraid of."

"I didn't imagine the piano music," I said. "I can hum the melody for you. And I didn't imagine the ghost. I can tell you just what she looked like."

"Let's talk about it next week," he said, climbing to his feet. "Our time is up. But until next time, I just want to assure you that your mind is perfectly normal. You're not crazy, Jerry. You shouldn't think that for a second."

He shook my hand. "You'll see," he said, opening the door for me. "You'll be amazed at what we figure out is behind that ghost of yours."

I muttered thanks and walked out of his office.

I made my way through the empty waiting room and stepped into the hallway.

And then I felt the ghost's icy grip tighten around my neck.

14

The unearthly cold shot through my entire body.

Uttering a terrified cry, I jerked away and spun around to face her.

"Mom!" I cried, my voice shrill and tiny.

"Sorry my hands are so cold," she replied calmly, unaware of how badly she had scared me. "It's *freezing* out. Didn't you hear me calling you?"

"No," I told her. My neck still tingled. I tried to rub the cold away. "I . . . uh . . . was thinking about stuff, and — "

"Well, I didn't mean to scare you," she said, leading the way across the small parking lot to the car. She stopped to pull the car keys from her bag. "Did you and Dr. Frye have a nice talk?"

"Kind of," I said.

This ghost has me jumping out of my skin, I realized as I climbed into the car. Now I'm seeing the ghost *everywhere*.

I have *got* to calm down, I told myself. I've just *got* to.

I've got to stop thinking that the ghost is following me.

But how?

Friday after school, Mom drove me to Dr. Shreek's music school. It was a cold, gray day. I stared at my breath steaming up the passenger window as we drove. It had snowed the day before, and the roads were still icy and slick.

"I hope we're not late," Mom fretted. We stopped for a light. She cleared the windshield in front of her with the back of her gloved hand. "I'm afraid to drive any faster than this."

All of the cars were inching along. We drove past a bunch of kids building a snow fort in a front yard. One little red-faced kid was crying because the others wouldn't let him join them.

"The school is practically in the next town," Mom remarked, pumping the brakes as we slid toward an intersection. "I wonder why Dr. Shreek has his school so far away from everything."

"I don't know," I answered dully. I was kind of nervous. "Do you think Dr. Shreek will be my instructor? Or do you think I'll have someone else?"

Mom shrugged her shoulders. She leaned forward over the steering wheel, struggling to see through the steamed-up windshield.

Finally, we turned onto the street where the school was located. I stared out at the block of dark, old houses. The houses gave way to woods, the bare trees tilting up under a white blanket of snow.

On the other side of the woods stood a brick building, half-hidden behind tall hedges. "This must be the school," Mom said, stopping the car in the middle of the street and staring up at the old building. "There's no sign or anything. But it's the only building for blocks."

"It's creepy-looking," I said.

Squinting through the windshield, she pulled the car into a narrow gravel driveway, nearly hidden by the tall, snow-covered hedges.

"Are you sure this is it?" I asked. I cleared a spot on the window with my hand and peered through it. The old building looked more like a prison than a school. It had rows of tiny windows above the ground floor, and the windows were all barred. Thick ivy covered the front of the building, making it appear even darker than it was.

"I'm pretty sure," Mom said, biting her lip. She lowered the window and stuck her head out, gazing up at the enormous, old house.

The sound of piano music floated into the car. Notes and scales and melodies all mixed together.

"Yeah. We've found it!" Mom declared happily.

"Go on, Jerry. Hurry. You're late. I'm going to go pick up something for dinner. I'll be back in an hour."

I pushed open the car door and stepped out onto the snowy driveway. My boots crunched loudly as I started to jog toward the building.

The piano music grew louder. Scales and songs jumbled together into a deafening rumble of noise.

A narrow walk led up to the front stoop. The walk hadn't been shoveled, and a layer of ice had formed under the snow. I slipped and nearly fell as I approached the entrance.

I stopped and gazed up. It looks more like a haunted house than a music school, I thought with a shiver.

Why did I have such a heavy feeling of dread?

Just nervous, I told myself.

Shrugging away my feeling, I turned the cold brass doorknob and pushed open the heavy door. It creaked open slowly. Taking a deep breath, I stepped into the school.

15

A long, narrow hall stretched before me. The hall was surprisingly dark. Coming in from the bright, white snow, it took my eyes a long time to adjust.

The walls were a dark tile. My boots thudded noisily on the hard floor. Piano notes echoed through the hall. The music seemed to burst out from all directions.

Where is Dr. Shreek's office? I wondered.

I made my way down the hall. The lights grew dimmer. I turned into another long hallway, and the piano music grew louder.

There were dark brown doors on both sides of this corridor. The doors had small, round windows in them. As I continued walking, I glanced into the windows.

I could see smiling instructors in each room, their heads bobbing in rhythm to piano music.

Searching for the office, I passed door after door. Each room had a student and an instructor.

The piano sounds became a roar, like an ocean of music crashing against the dark tile walls.

Dr. Shreek really has a lot of students, I thought. There must be a hundred pianos playing at once!

I turned another corner and then another.

I suddenly realized I had completely lost my sense of direction. I had no idea where I was. I couldn't find my way back to the front door if I wanted to!

"Dr. Shreek, where are you?" I muttered to myself. My voice was drowned out by the booming piano music that echoed off the walls and low ceiling.

I began to feel a little frightened.

What if these dark halls twisted on forever? I imagined myself walking and walking for the rest of my life, unable to find my way out, deafened by the pounding piano music.

"Jerry, stop scaring yourself," I said aloud.

Something caught my eye. I stopped walking and stared up at the ceiling. A small, black camera was perched above my head.

It appeared to be a video camera, like the security cameras you see in banks and stores.

Was someone watching me on a TV screen somewhere?

If they were, why didn't they come help me find the way to Dr. Shreek?

I began to get angry. What kind of school *was* this? No signs. No office. No one to greet people.

As I turned another corner, I heard a strange thumping sound. At first I thought it was just another piano in one of the practice rooms.

The thumping grew louder, closer. I stopped in the middle of the hall and listened. A high-pitched whine rose up over the thumping sounds.

Louder. Louder.

The floor seemed to shake.

And as I stared down the dark hall, an enormous monster turned the corner. Its huge, square body glowed in the dim light as if it were made of metal. Its rectangular head bobbed near the ceiling.

Its feet crashed against the hard floor as it moved to attack me. Eyes on the sides of its head flashed an angry red.

"No!" I cried, swallowing hard.

It uttered its high-pitched whine in reply. Then it lowered its gleaming head as if preparing for battle.

I spun away, determined to escape.

To my shock, as I turned, I saw Dr. Shreek.

He stood just a few yards down the hall. Dr. Shreek was watching the enormous creature move in on me, a pleased grin on his face.

16

I stopped short with a loud gasp.

Behind me, the creature was stomping closer, blasting out its angry whine.

Ahead of me, Dr. Shreek, his blue eyes glowing with pleasure, blocked my escape.

I cried out, preparing to be caught from behind by the silvery monster.

But it stopped.

Silence.

No crashing of its heavy metallic feet. No shrill whine.

"Hello, Jerry," Dr. Shreek said calmly, still grinning. "What are you doing all the way back here?"

Breathing hard, I pointed to the monster, which stood silently, staring down at me. "I — I — "

"You are admiring our floor sweeper?" Dr. Shreek asked.

"Your *what*?" I managed to choke out.

"Our floor sweeper. It *is* rather special," Dr. Shreek said. He stepped past me and put a hand on the front of the thing.

"It — it's a machine?" I stammered.

He laughed. "You didn't think it was alive, did you?"

I just gaped at it. I was still too freaked out to speak.

"Mr. Toggle, our janitor, built this for us," Dr. Shreek said, rubbing his hand along the square metal front of it. "It works like a dream. Mr. Toggle can build anything. He's a genius, a true genius."

"Wh-why does it have a face?" I asked, hanging back against the wall. "Why does it have eyes that light up?"

"Just Mr. Toggle's sense of humor," Dr. Shreek replied, chuckling. "He put in those cameras, too." He pointed to the video camera perched on the ceiling. "Mr. Toggle is a mechanical genius. We couldn't do a thing without him. We really couldn't."

I took a few reluctant steps forward and admired the floor sweeper from closer up. "I — I couldn't find your office," I told Dr. Shreek. "I was wandering and wandering — "

"I apologize," he replied quickly. "Let us begin your lesson. Come."

I followed him as he led the way back in the

direction I had come. He walked stiffly but rapidly. His white shirt was untucked in front of his big stomach. He swung his hands stiffly as he walked.

I felt really stupid. Imagine letting myself be terrified by a floor sweeper!

He pushed open one of the brown doors with a round window, and I followed him into the room. I glanced quickly around. It was a small, square room lighted by two rows of fluorescents on the ceiling. There was no window.

The only furniture was a small, brown upright piano, a narrow piano bench, and a music stand.

Dr. Shreek motioned for me to sit down on the piano bench, and we began our lesson. He stood behind me, placing my fingers carefully on the keys, even though I now knew how to do it myself.

We practiced different notes. I hit C's and D's. Then we tried E's and F's. He showed me my first chord. Then he had me do scales over and over.

"Excellent!" he declared near the end of the hour. "Excellent work, Jerry. I'm most pleased." His Santa Claus cheeks were bright pink beneath his white mustache.

I squeezed my hands together, trying to get rid of a cramp. "Are you going to be my teacher?" I asked.

He nodded. "Yes, I will instruct you in the basics," he replied. "Then when your hands are ready, you will be given over to one of our fine teachers."

"When my hands are ready?"

What exactly did he mean by that?

"Let us try this short piece," he said, reaching over me to turn the page in the music book. "Now, this piece has only three notes. But you must pay attention to the quarter notes and the half notes. Do you remember how long to continue a half note?"

I demonstrated on the piano. Then I tried to play the short melody. I did pretty well. Only a few clunkers.

"Wonderful! Wonderful!" Dr. Shreek declared, staring at my hands as I played. He glanced at his watch. "I'm afraid our time is up. See you next Friday, Jerry. Be sure to practice what I showed you."

I thanked him and climbed to my feet. I was glad the lesson was over. Having to concentrate so hard was really tiring. Both my hands were sweating, and I still had a cramp in one.

I headed to the door, then stopped. "Which way do I go?" I asked. "How do I get to the front?"

Dr. Shreek was busy collecting the work sheets

we had used, tucking them into the music book. "Just keep going left," he said without looking up. "You can't miss it."

I said good-bye and stepped out into the dark hallway. My ears were immediately attacked by the roar of piano notes.

Aren't the other lessons over? I wondered.

How come they keep playing even though the hour is up?

I glanced in both directions, making sure there were no floor sweepers waiting to attack. Then I turned left, as Dr. Shreek had instructed, and began to follow the hallway toward the front.

As I passed door after door, I could see the smiling instructors inside each room, their heads moving in rhythm with the piano playing.

Most of the students in these rooms were more advanced than me, I realized. They weren't practicing notes and scales. They were playing long, complicated pieces.

I turned left, then when the corridor came to an end, turned left one more time.

It took me a while to realize that I was lost again.

Had I missed a left turn somewhere?

The dark halls with their rows of brown doors on both sides all looked alike.

I turned left again. My heart began to pound.

Why wasn't anyone else in the hall?

Then up ahead I saw double doors. The front exit must be through those doors, I decided.

I made my way eagerly to the double doors and started to push through them — when powerful hands grabbed me from behind, and a gruff voice rasped in my ear, "No, you don't!"

17

"Huh?" I uttered a startled cry.

The hands pulled me back, then let go of my shoulders.

The double doors swung back into place.

I spun around to see a tall, wiry man with long, scraggly black hair and a stubbly black beard. He wore a yellow T-shirt under denim overalls.

"Not that way," he said softly. "You're looking for the front? It's up there." He pointed to the hall to the left.

"Oh. Sorry," I said, breathing hard. "You . . . scared me."

The man apologized. "I'll take you to the front," he offered, scratching his stubbly cheek. "Allow me to introduce myself. I'm Mr. Toggle."

"Oh. Hi," I said. "I'm Jerry Hawkins. Dr. Shreek told me about you. I — I saw your floor sweeper."

He smiled. His black eyes lit up like dark coals. "It's a beauty, isn't it? I have a few other creations like it, some even better."

"Dr. Shreek says you're a mechanical genius," I gushed.

Mr. Toggle chuckled to himself. "Yes. I programmed him to say that!" he joked. We both laughed.

"Next time you come to the school, I'll show you some of my other inventions," Mr. Toggle offered, adjusting his overall straps over his slender shoulders.

"Thanks," I replied. The front door was right up ahead. I was never so glad to see a door! "I'm sure I'll catch on to the layout of this place," I said.

He didn't seem to hear me. "Dr. Shreek tells me you have excellent hands," he said, a strange smile forming under his stubbly black beard. "That's what we look for here, Jerry. That's what we look for."

Feeling kind of awkward, I thanked him. I mean, what are you supposed to say when someone tells you what excellent hands you've got?

I pushed open the heavy front door and saw Mom waiting in the car. "Good night!" I called, and eagerly ran out of the school, into the snowy evening.

* * *

83

After dinner, Mom and Dad insisted that I show them what I had learned in my piano lesson. I really didn't want to. I had only learned that one simple song, and I still hadn't played it all the way through without goofing it up.

But they forced me into the family room and pushed me onto the piano bench. "If I'm going to pay for the lessons, I want to hear what you're learning," Dad said. He sat down close to Mom on the couch, facing the back of the piano.

"We only tried one song," I said. "Couldn't we wait till I learn more?"

"Play it," Dad ordered.

I sighed. "I have a cramp in my hand."

"Come on, Jerry. Don't make excuses," Mom snapped impatiently. "Just play the song, okay? Then we won't bug you anymore tonight."

"What did the school look like?" Dad asked Mom. "It's way on the other side of town, isn't it?"

"It's practically out of town," Mom told him. "It's in this very old house. Kind of run-down looking, actually. But Jerry told me it's nice inside."

"No, I didn't," I interrupted. "I said it was big. I didn't say it was nice. I got lost in the halls twice!"

Dad laughed. "I see you have your mother's sense of direction!"

Mom gave Dad a playful shove. "Just play the piece," she said to me.

I found it in the music book and propped the book in front of me on the piano. Then I arranged my fingers on the keys and prepared to play.

But before I hit the first note, the piano erupted with a barrage of low notes. It sounded as if someone was pounding on the keys with both fists.

"Jerry — stop it," Mom said sharply. "That's too loud."

"That can't be what you learned," Dad added.

I set my fingers in place and began to play.

But my notes were drowned out by the horrible, loud banging again.

It sounded like a little kid pounding away on the keys as hard as he could.

"Jerry — give us a *break*!" Mom shouted, holding her ears.

"But I'm not *doing* it!" I screamed. "It isn't *me*!"

18

They didn't believe me.

Instead, they got angry. They accused me of never taking anything seriously, and sent me up to my room.

I was actually glad to get out of the family room and away from that haunted piano. I knew who was pounding the keys and making that racket. The ghost was doing it.

Why? What was she trying to prove?

What did she plan to do to me?

Those questions I couldn't answer . . . yet.

The next Friday afternoon, Mr. Toggle kept his promise. He greeted me at the door to the piano school after my mom dropped me off. He led me through the twisting halls to his enormous workshop.

Mr. Toggle's workshop was the size of an auditorium. The vast room was cluttered with machines and electronic equipment.

An enormous two-headed metal creature, at least three times as tall as the floor sweeper that had terrified me the week before, stood in the center. It was surrounded by tape machines, stacks of electric motors, cases of tools and strange-looking parts, video equipment, a pile of bicycle wheels, several piano frames with no insides, animal cages, and an old car with its seats removed.

One entire wall seemed to be a control panel. It had more than a dozen video screens, all on, all showing different classes going on in the school. Around the screens were thousands of dials and knobs, blinking red and green lights, speakers, and microphones.

Beneath the control panel, on a counter that ran the length of the room, stood at least a dozen computers. All of them seemed to be powered up.

"Wow!" I exclaimed. My eyes kept darting from one amazing thing to another. "I don't *believe* this!"

Mr. Toggle chuckled. His dark eyes lit up. "I find ways to keep busy," he said. He led me to an uncluttered corner of the enormous room. "Let me show you some of my musical instruments."

He walked to a row of tall, gray metal cabinets

along the far wall. He pulled a few items from a cabinet and came hurrying back.

"Do you know what this is, Jerry?" He held up a shiny, brass instrument attached to some kind of tank.

"A saxophone?" I guessed.

"A very special saxophone," he said, grinning. "See? It's attached to this tank of compressed air. That means you don't have to blow into it. You can concentrate on your fingering."

"Wow," I said. "That's really neat."

"Here. Put this on," Mr. Toggle urged. He slipped a brown leather cap over my head. The cap had several thin wires flowing out the back, and it was attached to a small keyboard.

"What is it?" I asked, adjusting the cap over my ears.

"Blink your eyes," Mr. Toggle instructed.

I blinked my eyes, and the keyboard played a chord. I moved my eyes from right to left. It played another chord. I winked one eye. It played a note.

"It's completely eye-controlled," Mr. Toggle said with pride. "No hands required."

"Wow," I repeated. I didn't know what else to say. This stuff was amazing!

Mr. Toggle glanced up at a row of clocks on the control panel wall. "You're late for class, Jerry.

Dr. Shreek will be waiting. Tell him it's my fault, okay?"

"Okay," I said. "Thanks for showing me everything."

He laughed. "I didn't show you *everything*," he joked. "There's lots more." He rubbed his stubbly beard. "But you'll see it all in due time."

I thanked him again and hurried toward the door. It was nearly four-fifteen. I hoped Dr. Shreek wouldn't be angry that I was fifteen minutes late.

As I jogged across the enormous workroom, I nearly ran into a row of dark metal cabinets, shut and padlocked.

Turning away from them, I suddenly heard a voice.

"Help!" A weak cry.

I stopped by the side of the cabinet and listened hard.

And heard it again. A little voice, very faint. "Help me, please!"

19

"Mr. Toggle — what's that?" I cried.

He had begun fiddling with the wires on the brown leather cap. He slowly looked up. "What's *what?*"

"That cry," I told him, pointing to the cabinet. "I heard a voice."

He frowned. "It's just damaged equipment," he muttered, returning his attention to the wires.

"Huh? Damaged equipment?" I wasn't sure I had heard him correctly.

"Yeah. Just some damaged equipment," he repeated impatiently. "You'd better hurry, Jerry. Dr. Shreek must be wondering where you are."

I heard a second cry. A voice, very weak and tiny. "Help me — please!"

I hesitated. Mr. Toggle was staring at me impatiently.

I had no choice. I turned and ran from the room, the weak cries still in my ears.

On Saturday afternoon I went outside to shovel snow off our driveway. It had snowed the night before, only an inch or two. Now it was one of those clear winter days with a bright blue sky overhead.

It felt good to be out in the crisp air, getting some exercise. Everything seemed so fresh and clean.

I was finishing down at the bottom of the drive, my arms starting to ache from all the shoveling, when I saw Kim Li Chin. She was climbing out of her mother's black Honda, carrying her violin case. I guessed she was coming from a lesson.

I had seen her in school a few times, but I hadn't really talked to her since that day she ran away from me in the hall.

"Hey!" I called across the street, leaning on the shovel, a little out of breath. "Hi!"

She handed the violin case to her mother and waved back. Then she came jogging toward me, her black hightops crunching over the snow. "How's it going?" she asked. "Pretty snow, huh?"

I nodded. "Yeah. Want to shovel some? I still have to do the walk."

She laughed. "No thanks." She had a high, tinkly laugh, like two glasses clinking together.

"You coming from a violin lesson?" I asked, still leaning on the shovel.

"Yeah. I'm working on a Bach piece. It's pretty hard."

"You're ahead of me," I told her. "I'm still doing mostly notes and scales."

Her smile faded. Her eyes grew thoughtful.

We talked a little while about school. Then I asked if she'd like to come in and have some hot chocolate or something.

"What about the walk?" she asked, pointing. "I thought you had to shovel it."

"Dad would be disappointed if I didn't save some of it for him," I joked.

Mom filled two big white mugs with hot chocolate. Of course I burned my tongue on the first sip.

Kim and I were sitting in the den. Kim sat on the piano bench and tapped some keys lightly. "It has a really good tone," she said, her face growing serious. "Better than my mother's piano."

"Why did you run away that afternoon?" I blurted out.

It had been on my mind ever since it happened. I *had* to know the answer.

She lowered her eyes to the piano keyboard and pretended she hadn't heard me.

So I asked again. "Why did you run away like that, Kim?"

"I didn't," she replied finally, still avoiding my eyes. "I was late for a lesson, that's all."

I set my hot chocolate mug down on the coffee table and leaned against the arm of the couch. "I told you I was going to take piano lessons at the Shreek School, remember? Then you got this strange look on your face, and you ran away."

Kim sighed. She had the white hot chocolate mug in her lap. I saw that she was gripping it tightly in both hands. "Jerry, I really don't want to talk about it," she said softly. "It's too . . . too scary."

"Scary?" I asked.

"Don't you *know* the stories about the Shreek School?" she asked.

20

I laughed. I'm not sure why. Maybe it was the serious expression on Kim's face. "Stories? What kind of stories?"

"I really don't want to tell you," she said. She took a long sip from the white mug, then returned it to her lap.

"I just moved here, remember?" I told her. "So I haven't heard any stories. What are they about?"

"Things about the school," she muttered. She climbed off the piano bench and walked to the window, carrying the mug in one hand.

"What kinds of things?" I demanded. "Come on, Kim — *tell* me!"

"Well . . . things like, there are monsters there," she replied, staring out the window into my snowy back yard. "Real monsters that live in the basement."

"Monsters?" I laughed.

Kim spun around. "It's not funny," she snapped.

94

"I've *seen* the monsters," I told her, shaking my head.

Her face filled with surprise. "You've *what*?"

"I've seen the monsters," I repeated. "They're floor sweepers."

"Huh?" Her mouth dropped open. She nearly spilled hot chocolate down the front of her sweatshirt. "Floor sweepers?"

"Yeah. Mr. Toggle built them. He works at the school. He's some kind of mechanical genius. He builds all kinds of things."

"But — " she started.

"I saw one my first day at the school," I continued. "I thought it was some kind of monster. It made this weird whining sound, and it was coming right at me. I practically dropped my teeth! But it was one of Mr. Toggle's floor cleaners."

Kim tilted her head, staring at me thoughtfully. "Well, you know how stories get started," she said. "I *knew* they probably weren't true. They probably all have simple explanations like that."

"All?" I asked. "There are more?"

"Well . . . " She hesitated. "There were stories about how kids went in for lessons and never came out again. How they vanished, just disappeared."

"That's impossible," I said.

"Yeah, I guess," she quickly agreed.

Then I remembered the tiny voice from the cabinet, calling out for help.

It *had* to be some invention of Mr. Toggle's, I told myself. It *had* to be.

Damaged equipment, he said. He didn't seem the least bit excited or upset about it.

"It's funny how scary stories get started," Kim said, walking back to the piano bench.

"Well, the piano school building is creepy and old," I said. "It really looks like some kind of haunted mansion. I guess that's probably why some of the stories got started."

"Probably," she agreed.

"The school isn't haunted, but that piano is!" I told her. I don't know what made me say it. I hadn't told anyone about the ghost and the piano. I knew no one would believe me.

Kim gave a little start and stared at the piano. "This piano is haunted? What do you mean? How do you know?"

"Late at night, I hear someone playing it," I told her. "A woman. I saw her once."

Kim laughed. "You're putting me on — right?"

I shook my head. "No, I'm serious, Kim. I saw this woman. Late at night. She plays the same sad melody over and over."

"Jerry, come on!" Kim pleaded, rolling her eyes.

"The woman talked to me. Her skin fell off. It — it was so frightening, Kim. Her face disappeared. Her skull, it stared at me. And she warned me to stay away. Stay away."

I felt a shiver. Somehow I had shut that scary scene out of my mind for a few days. But now, as I told it to Kim, it all came back to me.

Kim had a big grin on her face. "You're a better storyteller than I am," she said. "Do you know a lot of ghost stories?"

"*It isn't a story!*" I cried. Suddenly, I was desperate for her to believe me.

Kim started to reply, but my mom poked her head into the family room and interrupted. "Kim, your mom just called. She needs you to come home now."

"Guess I'd better go," Kim said, setting down the hot chocolate mug.

I followed her out.

We had just reached the family room doorway when the piano began to play. A strange jumble of notes.

"See?" I cried excitedly to Kim. "See? *Now* do you believe me?"

21

We both turned back to stare at the piano.

Bonkers was strutting over the keys, her tail straight up behind her.

Kim laughed. "Jerry, you're funny! I almost believed you!"

"But — but — " I sputtered.

That stupid cat had made a fool of me again.

"See you in school," Kim said. "I loved your ghost story."

"Thanks," I said weakly. Then I hurried across the room to chase Bonkers off the piano.

Late that night I heard the piano playing again.

I sat straight up in bed. The shadows on my ceiling seemed to be moving in time to the music.

I had been sleeping lightly, restlessly. I must have kicked off my covers in my sleep, because they were bunched at the foot of the bed.

Now, listening to the familiar slow melody, I was wide awake.

This was not Bonkers strutting over the keys. This was the ghost.

I stood up. The floorboards were ice-cold. Outside the bedroom window, I could see the winter-bare trees shivering in a strong breeze.

As I crept to the bedroom doorway, the music grew louder.

Should I go down there? I asked myself.

Will the ghost disappear the minute I poke my head into the family room?

Do I really want to see her?

I didn't want to see that hideous, grinning skull again.

But I realized I couldn't just stand there in the doorway. I couldn't go back to bed. I couldn't ignore it.

I *had* to go investigate.

I was pulled downstairs, as if tugged by an invisible rope.

Maybe this time Mom and Dad will hear her, too, I thought as I made my way along the hallway. Maybe they will see her, too. Maybe they will finally believe me.

Kim flashed into my mind as I started down the creaking stairs. She thought I was making up a ghost story. She thought I was trying to be funny.

But there really was a ghost in my house, a ghost playing my piano. And I was the only one who knew it.

Into the living room. Across the worn carpet to the dining room.

The music floated so gently, so quietly.

Such ghostly music, I thought. . . .

I hesitated just short of the family room doorway. Would she vanish the instant I peeked in?

Was she *waiting* for me?

Taking a deep breath, I took a step into the family room.

22

She had her head down, her long hair falling over her face.

I couldn't see her eyes.

The piano music seemed to swirl around me, pulling me closer despite my fear.

My legs were trembling, but I took a step closer. Then another.

She was all gray. Shades of gray against the blackness of the night sky through the windows.

Her head bobbed and swayed in rhythm with the music. The sleeves of her blouse billowed as her arms moved over the keys.

I couldn't see her eyes. I couldn't see her face. Her long hair covered her, as if hiding her behind a curtain.

The music soared, so sad, so incredibly sad.

I took a step closer. I suddenly realized I had forgotten to breathe. I let my breath out in a loud *whoosh.*

She stopped playing. Maybe the sound of my breathing alerted her that I was there.

As she raised her head, I could see her pale eyes peering out at me through her hair.

I didn't move.

I didn't breathe.

I didn't make a sound.

"The stories are true," she whispered. A dry whisper that seemed to come from far away.

I wasn't sure I had heard her correctly. I tried to say something, but my voice caught in my throat.

No sound came out at all.

"The stories are true," she repeated. Her voice was only air, a hiss of air.

I goggled at her.

"Wh-what stories?" I finally managed to choke out.

"The stories about the school," she answered, her hair falling over her face. Then she started to raise her arms off the piano keys. *"They're true,"* she moaned. *"The stories are true."*

She held her arms up to me.

Gaping at them in horror, I cried out — then started to gag.

Her arms ended in stumps. She had no hands.

23

The next thing I knew, my mom was wrapping her arms around me. "Jerry, calm down. Jerry, it's okay. It's okay," she kept repeating.

"Huh? Mom?"

I was gasping for breath. My chest was heaving up and down. My legs were all wobbly.

"Mom? Where — ? How — ?"

I looked up to see my dad standing a few feet away, squinting at me through his glasses, his arms crossed in front of his bathrobe. "Jerry, you were screaming loud enough to wake the entire town!"

I stared at him in disbelief. I hadn't even realized I was screaming.

"It's okay now," Mom said soothingly. "It's okay, Jerry. You're okay now."

I'm okay?

Again, I pictured the ghost woman, all in gray, her hair falling down, forming a curtain over her face. Again, I saw her raise her arms to show me. Again, I saw the horrible stumps where her hands should have been.

And again, I heard her dry whisper, *"The stories are true."*

Why didn't she have any hands? Why?

How did she play the piano without hands?

Why was she haunting my piano? Why did she want to terrify me?

The questions circled my brain so fast, I wanted to scream and scream and scream. But I was all screamed out.

"Your mom and I were both sound asleep. You scared us to death," Dad said. "I never heard wails like that."

I didn't remember screaming. I didn't remember the ghost disappearing, or Mom and Dad rushing in.

It was too horrifying. I guess my mind just shut off.

"I'll make you some hot chocolate," Mom said, still holding me tight. "Try to stop trembling."

"I — I'm trying," I stammered.

"Guess it was another nightmare," I heard Dad tell Mom. "Must have been a vivid one."

"It wasn't a nightmare!" I shrieked.

"Sorry," Dad said quickly. He didn't want to get me started again.

But it was too late. Before I even realized it

was happening, I started to scream. "I don't want to play the piano! Get it out of here! Get it out!"

"Jerry, please — " Mom pleaded, her face tight with alarm.

But I couldn't stop. "I don't want to play! I don't want lessons! I won't go to that piano school! I won't, I *won't!*"

"Okay, okay!" Dad cried, shouting to be heard over my desperate wails. "Okay, Jerry. No one is going to force you."

"Huh?" I gazed from one parent to the other, trying to see if they were serious.

"If you don't want piano lessons, you don't have to take them," Mom said, keeping her voice in a low, soothing tone. "You're only signed up for one more anyway."

"Yeah," Dad quickly joined in. "When you go to the school on Friday, just tell Dr. Shreek that it's your last lesson."

"But I don't want — " I started.

Mom put a gentle hand over my mouth. "You have to tell Dr. Shreek, Jerry. You can't just quit."

"Tell him on Friday," Dad urged. "You don't have to play the piano if you don't want to. Really."

Mom's eyes searched mine. "Does that make you feel better, Jerry?"

I glanced at the piano, now silent, shimmering

dully in the dim light from overhead. "Yeah. I guess," I muttered uncertainly. "I guess it does."

Friday afternoon after school, a gray, blustery day with dark snowclouds hovering low overhead, Mom drove me to the piano school. She pulled into the long driveway between the tall hedges and stopped in front of the entrance to the dark, old building.

I hesitated. "Couldn't I just run in and tell Dr. Shreek that I quit, then run right back out?"

Mom glanced at the clock on the dashboard. "Take one more lesson, Jerry. It won't hurt. We've already paid for it."

I sighed unhappily. "Will you come in with me? Or can you wait out here for me?"

Mom frowned. "Jerry, I've got three stops to make. I'll be back in an hour, I promise."

Reluctantly, I pushed open the car door. "Bye, Mom."

"If Dr. Shreek asks why you're quitting, just tell him it was interfering with your schoolwork."

"Okay. See you in an hour," I said. I slammed the car door, then watched as she drove away, the tires crunching over the gravel drive.

I turned and trudged into the school building.

My sneakers thudded loudly as I made my way through the dark halls to Dr. Shreek's room. I looked for Mr. Toggle, but didn't see him. Maybe he was in his enormous workshop inventing more amazing things.

The usual roar of piano notes poured from the practice rooms as I passed by them. Through the small, round windows I could see smiling instructors, their hands waving, keeping the beat, their heads swaying to their students' playing.

As I turned a corner and headed down another long, dark corridor, a strange thought popped into my head. I suddenly realized that I had never seen another student in the halls.

I had seen instructors through the windows of the rooms. And I had heard the noise of their students' playing. But I had never seen another student.

Not one.

I didn't have long to think about it. A smiling Dr. Shreek greeted me outside the door to our practice room. "How are you today, Jerry?"

"Okay," I replied, following him into the room.

He wore baggy gray pants held up with bright red suspenders over a rumpled white shirt. His white hair looked as if it hadn't been brushed in a few days. He motioned for me to take my place on the piano bench.

I sat down quickly, folding my hands tensely in my lap. I wanted to get my speech over with quickly before we began the lesson. "Uh . . . Dr. Shreek?"

He walked stiffly across the small room until he was standing right in front of me. "Yes, my boy?" he beamed down at me, his Santa Claus cheeks bright pink.

"Well . . . I . . . this will be my last lesson," I choked out. "I've decided I . . . uh . . . have to quit."

His smile vanished. He grabbed my wrist. "Oh, no," he said, lowering his voice to a growl. "No. You're not leaving, Jerry."

"Huh?" I cried.

He tightened his grip on my wrist. He was really hurting me.

"Quitting?" he exclaimed. "Not with those hands." His face twisted into an ugly snarl. "You can't quit, Jerry. I need those beautiful hands."

24

"Let go!" I screamed.

He ignored me and tightened his grip, his eyes narrowing menacingly. "Such excellent hands," he muttered. "Excellent."

"No!"

With a shrill cry, I jerked my wrist free. I leapt up from the piano bench and began running to the door.

"Come back, Jerry!" Dr. Shreek called angrily. "You cannot get away!"

He started after me, moving stiffly but steadily, taking long strides.

I pushed open the door and darted out into the hall. The banging of piano music greeted my ears. The long, dark hall was empty as always.

"Come back, Jerry!" Dr. Shreek called from right behind me.

"No!" I cried out again. I hesitated, trying to decide which way to go, which way led to the front door. Then I lowered my head and started to run.

My sneakers thudded over the hard floor. I ran as fast as I could, faster than I'd ever run in my life. The practice rooms whirred past in a dark blur.

But to my surprise, Dr. Shreek kept right behind me. "Come back, Jerry," he called, not even sounding out of breath. "Come back. You cannot get away from me."

Glancing back, I saw that he was gaining on me.

I could feel the panic rise to my throat, choking off my air. My legs ached. My heart pounded so hard, it felt as if my chest were about to burst.

I turned a corner and ran down another long hall.

Where was I? Was I heading toward the front door?

I couldn't tell. This dark hallway looked like all the others.

Maybe Dr. Shreek is right. Maybe I *can't* get away, I thought, feeling the blood throb at my temples as I turned another corner.

I searched for Mr. Toggle. Perhaps he could save me. But the halls were empty. Piano music poured out of every room, but no one was out in the hall.

"Come back, Jerry! There's no use running!"

"Mr. Toggle!" I screamed, my voice hoarse and

breathless. "Mr. Toggle — help me! Help me, please!"

I turned another corner, my sneakers sliding on the smoothly polished floor. I was gasping for breath now, my chest heaving.

I saw double doors up ahead. Did they lead to the front?

I couldn't remember.

With a low moan, I stuck out both hands and pushed open the doors.

"No!" I heard Dr. Shreek shout behind me. "No, Jerry! Don't go into the recital hall!"

Too late.

I pushed through the doors and bolted inside. Still running, I found myself in an enormous, brightly lit room.

I took a few more steps — then stopped in horror.

The piano music was deafening — like a never-ending roar of thunder.

At first, the room was a blur. Then it slowly began to come into focus.

I saw row after row of black pianos. Beside each piano stood a smiling instructor. The instructors all looked alike. They all were bobbing their heads in time to the music.

The music was being played by —

It was being played by —

I gasped, staring from row to row.
The music was being played by — *HANDS!*
Human hands floating over the keyboards.
No people attached.
Just *HANDS!*

25

My eyes darted down the rows of pianos. A pair of hands floated above each piano.

The instructors were all bald-headed men in gray suits with smiles plastered on their faces. Their heads bobbed and swayed, their gray eyes opened and closed as the hands played over the keyboards.

Hands.

Just hands.

As I gaped, paralyzed, trying to make sense of what I saw, Dr. Shreek burst into the room from behind me. He made a running dive at my legs, trying to tackle me.

Somehow I dodged away from his outstretched hands.

He groaned and hit the floor on his stomach. I watched him slide across the smooth floor, his face red with anger.

Then I spun around, away from the dozens of

hands, away from the banging pianos, and started back toward the doors.

But Dr. Shreek was faster than I imagined. To my surprise, he was on his feet in a second, moving quickly to block my escape.

I skidded to a stop.

I tried to turn around, to get away from him. But I lost my balance and fell.

The piano music swirled around me. I looked up to see the rows of hands pounding away on their keyboards.

With a frightened gasp, I struggled to my feet. Too late.

Dr. Shreek was closing in on me, a gleeful smile of triumph on his red, round face.

26

"No!" I cried, and tried to climb to my feet.

But Dr. Shreek bent over me, grabbed my left ankle, and held on. "You can't get away, Jerry," he said calmly, not even out of breath.

"Let me go! Let me go!" I tried to twist out of his grip. But he was surprisingly strong. I couldn't free myself.

"Help me! Somebody — help me!" I cried, screaming over the roar of the pianos.

"I need your hands, Jerry," Dr. Shreek said. "Such beautiful hands."

"You can't! You *can't!*" I shrieked.

The double doors burst open.

Mr. Toggle ran in, his expression confused. His eyes darted quickly around the enormous room.

"Mr. Toggle!" I cried happily. "Mr. Toggle — help me! He's *crazy*! Help me!"

Mr. Toggle's mouth dropped open in surprise. "Don't worry, Jerry!" he called.

"Help me! Hurry!" I screamed.

"Don't worry!" he repeated.

"Jerry, you can't get away!" Dr. Shreek cried, holding me down on the floor.

Struggling to free myself, I watched Mr. Toggle run to the far wall. He pulled open a gray metal door, revealing some kind of control panel.

"Don't worry!" he called to me.

I saw him pull a switch on the control panel.

Instantly, Dr. Shreek's hand loosened.

I pulled my leg free and scrambled to my feet, panting hard.

Dr. Shreek slumped into a heap. His hands drooped lifelessly to his sides. His eyes closed. His head sank, his chin lowering to his chest.

He didn't move.

He's some kind of robot, I saw to my amazement.

"Are you okay, Jerry?" Mr. Toggle had hurried to my side.

I suddenly realized my entire body was trembling. The piano music roared inside my head. The room began to spin.

I held my hands over my ears, trying to shut out the pounding noise. "Make them stop! Tell them to stop!" I cried.

Mr. Toggle jogged back to the control panel and threw another switch.

The music stopped. The hands froze in place

over their keyboards. The instructors stopped bobbing their heads.

"Robots. All robots," I murmured, still shaking.

Mr. Toggle hurried back, his dark eyes studying me. "You're okay?"

"Dr. Shreek — he's a robot," I uttered in a trembling whisper. If only I could get my knees to stop shaking!

"Yes, he's my best creation," Mr. Toggle declared, smiling. He placed a hand on Dr. Shreek's still shoulder. "He's really lifelike, isn't he?"

"They — they're *all* robots," I whispered, motioning to the instructors, frozen beside their pianos.

Mr. Toggle nodded. "Primitive ones," he said, still leaning on Dr. Shreek. "They're not as advanced as my buddy Dr. Shreek here."

"You — made them all?" I asked.

Mr. Toggle nodded, smiling. "Every one of them."

I couldn't stop shaking. I was starting to feel really sick. "Thanks for stopping him. I guess Dr. Shreek was out of control or something. I — I've got to go now," I said weakly. I started walking toward the double doors, forcing my trembling knees to cooperate.

"Not just yet," Mr. Toggle said, placing a gentle hand on my shoulder.

"Huh?" I turned to face him.

"You can't leave just yet," he said, his smile fading. "I need your hands, see."

"What?"

He pointed to a piano against the wall. A gray-suited instructor stood lifelessly beside it, a smile frozen on his face. There were no hands suspended over the keyboard.

"That will be *your* piano, Jerry," Mr. Toggle said.

27

I started backing toward the double doors one step at a time. "Wh-why?" I stammered. "Why do you need my hands?"

"Human hands are too hard to build, too complicated, too many parts," Mr. Toggle replied. He scratched his black, stubbly beard with one hand as he moved toward me.

"But — " I started, taking another step back.

"I can make the hands play beautifully," Mr. Toggle explained, his eyes locked on mine. "I've designed computer programs to make them play more beautifully than any live human can play. But I can't build hands. The students must supply the hands."

"But *why*?" I demanded. "Why are you *doing* this?"

"To make beautiful music, naturally," Mr. Toggle replied, taking another step closer. "I love beautiful music, Jerry. And music is so much more beautiful, so much more *perfect*, when human mistakes don't get in the way."

He took another step toward me. Then another. "You understand, don't you?" His dark eyes burned into mine.

"No!" I screamed. "No, I *don't* understand! You can't have my hands! You can't!"

I took another step back. My legs were still trembling.

If I can just get through those doors, I thought, maybe I have a chance. Maybe I can outrun him. Maybe I can get out of this crazy building.

It was my only hope.

Gathering my strength, ignoring the pounding of my heart, I turned.

I darted toward the doors.

"Ohh!" I cried out as the ghost woman appeared in front of me.

The woman from my house, from my piano.

She rose up, all in gray except for her eyes. Her eyes glowed red as fire. Her mouth was twisted in an ugly snarl of rage. She floated toward me, blocking my path to the door.

I'm trapped, I realized.

Trapped between Mr. Toggle and the ghost.

There's no escape now.

28

"I warned you!" the ghost woman wailed, her red eyes glowing with fury. *"I warned you!"*

"No, please — " I managed to cry in a choked voice. I raised my hands in front of me, trying to shield myself from her. "Please — let me go!"

To my surprise, she floated right past me.

She was glaring at Mr. Toggle, I realized.

He staggered back, his face tight with terror.

The ghost woman raised her arms. *"Awaken!"* she wailed. *"Awaken!"*

And as she waved her arms, I saw a fluttering at the pianos. The fluttering became a mist. Wisps of gray cloud rose up from each piano.

I backed up to the doors, my eyes wide with disbelief.

At each piano, the dark mist took shape.

They were ghosts, I realized.

Ghosts of boys, girls, men, and women.

I watched, frozen in horror, as they rose up and

claimed their hands. They moved their fingers, testing their hands.

And then, with arms outstretched, their hands fluttering in front of them, the ghosts floated away from their pianos, moving in rows, in single file, toward Mr. Toggle.

"No! Get away! Get away!" Mr. Toggle shrieked.

He turned and tried to flee through the doors. But I blocked his path.

And the ghosts swarmed over him.

Their hands pulled him down. Their hands pressed him to the floor.

He kicked and struggled and screamed.

"Let me up! Get off me! Get off!"

But the hands, dozens and dozens of hands, flattened over him, held him down, pushed him face-down on the floor.

The gray ghost woman turned to me. *"I tried to warn you!"* she called over Mr. Toggle's frantic screams. *"I tried to scare you away! I lived in your house. I was a victim of this school! I tried to frighten you from becoming a victim, too!"*

"I — I — "

"Run!" she ordered. *"Hurry — call for help!"*

But I was frozen in place, too shocked by what I was seeing to move.

As I stared in disbelief, the ghostly hands swarmed over Mr. Toggle and lifted him off the floor. He squirmed and struggled, but he couldn't free himself from their powerful grasp.

They carried him to the door and then out. I followed to the doorway to watch.

Mr. Toggle appeared to be floating, floating into the deep woods beside the school. The hands carried him away. He disappeared into the tangled trees.

I knew he'd never be seen again.

I spun around to thank the ghost woman for trying to warn me.

But she was gone, too.

I was all alone now.

The hall stretched behind me in eerie silence. Ghostly silence.

The piano music had ended . . . forever.

A few weeks later, my life had pretty much returned to normal.

Dad put an ad in the newspaper and sold the piano right away to a family across town. It left a space in the family room, so Mom and Dad got a big-screen TV!

I never saw the ghost woman again. Maybe she moved out with the piano. I don't know.

I made some good friends and was starting to get used to my new school. I was thinking seriously of trying out for the baseball team.

I'm not a great hitter, but I'm good in the field.

Everyone says I have great hands.

Add *more*

Goosebumps®

to your collection . . .

Here's a chilling preview of

A NIGHT IN TERROR TOWER

5

"Ohhhh." A horrified moan escaped Eddie's throat as he gaped at the cuff around my wrist. His mouth dropped open, and his chin started to quiver.

"Help me!" I wailed, thrashing my arm frantically, tugging at the chain. "Get me out of this!"

Eddie turned as white as a ghost.

I couldn't keep a straight face any longer. I started to laugh. And I slid the handcuff off my wrist.

"Gotcha back!" I jeered. "That's for stealing my camera. Now we're even!"

"I — I — I —" Eddie sputtered. His dark eyes glowered at me angrily. "I really thought you were hurt," he muttered. "Don't do that again, Sue. I mean it."

I stuck my tongue out at him. I know it wasn't very mature. My brother doesn't always bring out the best in me.

"Follow me, please!" Mr. Starkes' voice echoed off the stone walls. Eddie and I moved closer as our tour group huddled around Mr. Starkes.

"We're going to climb the stairs to the north tower now," the tour guide announced. "As you will see, the stairs are quite narrow and steep. So we will have to go single file. Please watch your step."

Mr. Starkes ducked his bald head as he led the way through a low, narrow doorway. Eddie and I were at the end of the line.

The stone stairs twisted up the Tower like a corkscrew. There was no handrailing. And the stairs were so steep and so twisty, I had to hold on to the wall to keep my balance as I climbed.

The air grew warmer as we made our way higher. So many feet had climbed these ancient stones, the stairs were worn smooth, the edges round.

I tried to imagine prisoners being marched up these stairs to the Tower. Their legs must have trembled with fear.

Up ahead, Eddie made his way slowly, peering up at the soot-covered stone walls. "It's too dark," he complained, turning back to me. "Hurry up, Sue. Don't get too far behind."

My coat brushed against the stone wall as I climbed. I'm pretty skinny, but the stairway was so narrow, I kept bumping the sides.

After climbing for what seemed like hours, we

stopped on a landing. Straight ahead of us was a small dark cell behind metal bars.

"This is a cell in which political prisoners were held," Mr. Starkes told us. "Enemies of the king were brought here. You can see it was not the most comfortable place in the world."

Moving closer, I saw that the cell contained only a small stone bench and a wooden writing table.

"What happened to these prisoners?" a white-haired woman asked Mr. Starkes. "Did they stay in this cell for years and years?"

"No," Mr. Starkes replied, rubbing his chin. "Most of them were beheaded."

I felt a chill at the back of my neck. I stepped up to the bars and peered into the small cell.

Real people stood inside this cell, I thought. Real people held on to these bars and stared out. Sat at that little writing table. Paced back and forth in that narrow space. Waiting to meet their fate.

Swallowing hard, I glanced at my brother. I could see that he was just as horrified as I was.

"We have not reached the top of the Tower yet," Mr. Starkes announced. "Let us continue our climb."

The stone steps became steeper as we made our way up the curving stairway. I trailed my hand along the wall as I followed Eddie up to the top.

And as I climbed, I suddenly had the strangest feeling — that I had been here before. That I had followed the twisting stairs. That I had climbed to the top of this ancient tower before.

Of course, that was impossible.

Eddie and I had never been to England before in our lives.

The feeling stayed with me as our tour group crowded into the tiny chamber at the top. Had I seen this tower in a movie? Had I seen pictures of it in a magazine?

Why did it look so familiar to me?

I shook my head hard, as if trying to shake away the strange, troubling thoughts. Then I stepped up beside Eddie and gazed around the tiny room.

A small round window high above our heads allowed a wash of gloomy gray light to filter down over us. The rounded walls were bare, lined with cracks and dark stains. The ceiling was low, so low that Mr. Starkes and some of the other adults had to duck their heads.

"Perhaps you can feel the sadness in this room," Mr. Starkes said softly.

We all huddled closer to hear him better. Eddie stared up at the window, his expression solemn.

"This is the tower room where a young prince and princess were brought," Mr. Starkes continued; speaking solemnly. "It was the early fifteenth century. The prince and princess — Edward and Susannah of York — were locked in this tiny tower cell."

He waved the red pennant in a circle. We all followed it, gazing around the small, cold room. "Imagine. Two children. Grabbed away from their home. Locked away in the drab chill of this cell in the top of a tower." Mr. Starkes' voice remained just above a whisper.

I suddenly felt cold. I zipped my coat back up. Eddie had his hands shoved deep in his jeans pockets. His eyes grew wide with fear as he gazed around the tiny, dark room.

"The prince and princess weren't up here for long," Mr. Starkes continued, lowering the pennant to his side. "That night while they slept, the Lord High Executioner and his men crept up the stairs. Their orders were to smother the two children. To keep the prince and princess from ever taking the throne."

Mr. Starkes shut his eyes and bowed his head. The silence in the room seemed to grow heavy.

No one moved. No one spoke.

The only sound was the whisper of wind through the tiny window above our heads.

I shut my eyes, too. I tried to picture a boy and a girl. Frightened and alone. Trying to sleep in this cold, stone room.

The door bursts open. Strange men break in. They don't say a word. They rush to smother the boy and girl.

Right in this room.

Right where I am standing now, I thought.

I opened my eyes. Eddie was gazing at me, his expression troubled. "This is . . . really scary," he whispered.

"Yeah," I agreed. Mr. Starkes started to tell us more.

But the camera fell out of my hand. It clattered noisily on the stone floor. I bent to pick it up. "Oh, look, Eddie — the lens broke!" I cried.

"Ssshhh! I missed what Mr. Starkes said about the prince and princess!" Eddie protested.

"But my camera —!" I shook it. I don't know why. It's not like shaking it would help fix the lens.

"What did he say? Did you hear?" Eddie demanded.

I shook my head. "Sorry. I missed it."

We walked over to a low cot against the wall. A three-legged wooden stool stood beside it. The only furniture in the chamber.

Did the prince and princess sit here? I wondered.

Did they stand on the bed and try to see out the window?

What did they talk about? Did they wonder what was going to happen to them? Did they talk about the fun things they would do when they were freed? When they returned home?

It was all so sad, so horribly sad.

I stepped up to the cot and rested my hand on it. It felt hard.

Black markings on the wall caught my eye. Writing?

Had the prince or the princess left a message on the wall?

I leaned over the cot and squinted at the markings.

No. No message. Just cracks in the stone.

"Sue — come on," Eddie urged. He tugged my arm.

"Okay, okay," I replied impatiently. I ran my hand over the cot again. It felt so lumpy and hard, so uncomfortable.

I gazed up at the window. The gray light had darkened to black. Dark as night out there.

The stone walls suddenly seemed to close in on me. I felt as if I were in a dark closet, a cold, frightening closet. I imagine the walls squeezing in, choking me, smothering me.

Is that how the prince and princess felt?

Was I feeling the same fear they had known over five hundred years ago?

With a heavy sigh, I let go of the cot and turned to Eddie. "Let's get out of here," I said in a trembling voice. "This room is just too frightening, too sad."

We turned away from the cot, took a few steps toward the stairs — and stopped.

"Hey —!" We both cried out in surprise.

Mr. Starkes and the tour group had disappeared.

6

"Where did they go?" Eddie cried in a shrill, startled voice. "They *left* us here!"

"They must be on their way back down the stairs," I told him. I gave him a gentle push. "Let's go."

Eddie lingered close to me. "You go first," he insisted quietly.

"You're not scared — are you?" I teased. "All alone in the Terror Tower?"

I don't know why I enjoy teasing my little brother so much. I *knew* he was scared. I was a little scared, too. But I couldn't help it.

As I said, Eddie doesn't always bring out the best in me.

I led the way to the twisting stairs. As I peered down, they seemed even darker and steeper.

"Why didn't we hear them leave?" Eddie demanded. "Why did they leave so fast?"

"It's late," I told him. "I think Mr. Starkes was eager to get everyone on the bus and back to their hotels. The Tower closes at five, I think." I glanced at my watch. It was five-twenty.

"Hurry," Eddie pleaded. "I don't want to be locked in. This place gives me the creeps."

"Me, too," I confessed.

Squinting into the darkness, I started down the steps. My sneakers slid on the smooth stone. Once again, I pressed one hand against the wall. It helped me keep my balance on the curving stairs.

"Where *are* they?" Eddie demanded nervously. "Why can't we hear the others on the stairs?"

The air grew cooler as we climbed lower. A pale yellow light washed over the landing just below us.

My hand swept through something soft and sticky. Cobwebs.

Yuck.

I could hear Eddie's rapid breathing behind me. "The bus will wait for us," I told him. "Just stay calm. Mr. Starkes won't drive off without us."

"Is anybody down there?" Eddie screamed. *"Can anybody hear me?"*

His shrill voice echoed down the narrow stone stairwell.

No reply.

"Where are the guards?" Eddie demanded.

"Eddie — please don't get worked up," I pleaded. "It's late. The guards are probably closing up. Mr. Starkes will be waiting for us down there. I promise you."

We stepped into the pale light of the landing. The small cell we had seen before stood against the wall.

"Don't stop," Eddie pleaded, breathing hard. "Keep going, Sue. Hurry!"

I put my hand on his shoulder to calm him. "Eddie, we'll be fine," I said soothingly. "We're almost down to the ground."

"But look —" Eddie protested. He pointed frantically.

I saw at once what was troubling him. There were *two* stairways leading down — one to the left of the cell, and one to the right.

"That's strange," I uttered, glancing from one to the other. "I don't remember a second stairway."

"Wh-which one is the right one?" he stammered.

I hesitated. "I'm not sure," I replied. I stepped over to the one on the right and peered down. I couldn't see very far because it curved so sharply.

"Which one? Which one?" Eddie repeated.

"I don't think it matters," I told him. "I mean, they both lead *down* — right?"

I motioned for him to follow me. "Come on. I think this is the one we took when we were climbing up."

I took one step down.

Then stopped.

I heard footsteps. Heavy footsteps. Coming *up* the stairs.

About the Author

R.L. STINE is the author of the series *Fear Street*, *Nightmare Room*, *Give Yourself Goosebumps*, and the phenomenally successful *Goosebumps*. His thrilling teen titles have sold more than 250 million copies internationally — enough to earn him a spot in the *Guinness Book of World Records*! Mr. Stine lives in New York City with his wife, Jane, and his son, Matt.

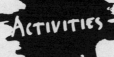